SUPER PAC
~~STRIKETHROUGH~~

Book 1 of the Parker Moore Series

SUPER PAC
~~STRIKETHROUGH~~

The first Super PAC wasn't about money.
A behind-the-scenes political thriller.

STEWERT JAMES

MITCHELL STREET PRESS
PETOSKEY, MICHIGAN

Mitchell Street Press
Petoskey, Michigan

www.stewertjames.com

DISCLAIMER: While the content of this book is based on actual experiences, details of some events have been fictionalized and some names have been changed to protect individual rights to privacy.

James, Stewert.
    Super PAC strikethrough / Stewert James. — Petoskey, Mich. : Mitchell Street Press, c2013.

    p. ; cm.
    (Parker Moore series ; book 1)
    ISBN: 978-0-9885011-0-2

        1. Political action committees—United States—21st century—Fiction.
2. Campaign funds—United States—Fiction. 3. Elections—United States—21st century—Fiction. 4. United States—Politics and government— 2009—Fiction.
5. Politicians—United States—Fiction. 6. Lobbying—United States—Fiction.
7. Foreign agents—United States—Fiction. 8. Abused husbands—Fiction.
9. Political fiction. I. Title. II. Series.

PS3610.A4547 S86 2013   2012951724

813/.6—dc23   1212

Printed in the United States of America
10 9 8 7 6 5 4 3 2 1

COVER & INTERIOR DESIGN BY TO THE POINT SOLUTIONS
www.tothepointsolutions.com

To my father. I would have been an orphan to the world.

Acknowledgments

As a poet, I always thank Nature and the Universe for material, time and space; however, as a novelist, I believe being a little more specific is justified.

I would like to thank my children, for their unwavering and steadfast courage and completeness they provide in my life.

I would like to thank John, for his frankness and unending stream of ideas as I wrote; also to Chad, for his careful critiques.

I thank the community in which I live. The warmth and love expressed by many has created a balance in life I've never before experienced.

Thanks to my editor, Mary Jo Zazueta, as a guide down a path never walked.

And finally, thank you to Christine. Her spirit, kindness, honesty, and most of all, love, has allowed me to blossom from a withered flower patch to a spreading garden of graces from which I give back to as many as I can every day of my life.

SUPER PAC
~~STRIKETHROUGH~~

"Living in a borderline personality world is like being in a floating bubble that hits and knocks around person to person and situation to situation. Pain feels good and anger is life giving. Those around you live in a dissociative haze making life bliss; afraid to break your bubble."

From a recovering borderline personality
who remains in intensive therapy (2009)

Chapter 1

The Middle
Petoskey, Michigan—Winter 2010

No one noticed the black Mercedes parked on a downtown street. Luxury cars were not out of the ordinary here. *When will they come out?* wondered the person sitting behind the wheel. A black-gloved hand was wrapped around the rosewood grips of a nickel-plated .357.

Piss on it. Can't wait. The door handle clicked open.

★   ★   ★

Parker stared at his cards, his glasses had slid down his nose. Sam sipped coffee with her right hand while her left held a confident row of spades and hearts. They were at their usual table at the Roast and Toast on Lake Street. It was January 2010. They were playing gin—one of their favorite pastimes—while they indulged in mugs of steaming coffee and fresh toast. They nodded and smiled good morning to the other customers.

This friendly atmosphere made the cozy coffee shop a comfort for the locals. Mary, the owner, said hello to everyone as she cleaned tables and made sure all had what they needed. A young couple with their arms wrapped around each other's waists sauntered in.

As they reviewed the breakfast menu, he whispered in her ear. The computer geeks sat in the back of the room, staring at screens while typing or reading. Their cell phones were out, to alert them to any incoming text messages. Jason replaced the oatmeal on the steam table with freshly made soups, while the rest of the staff, adorned in an assortment of curls, piercings, and tattoos, followed the routine of cooking and cleaning as though programmed by Bob Fosse in the 1960s.

★   ★   ★

Blair was on the second floor of the Michigan Library in Lansing. He was working on his laptop. As a private investment counselor, he liked to work in different venues depending on his mood. Today it was a professorial mood since the project was for a professor at the University of Michigan. The tables were stationed in rows between the stacks of books. Small, blue desk lamps gave a false pretense to the normal quiet, as scads of children created a cacophony below; their laughter and yelling echoing through the stairwells and hallways.

A few blocks to the east, the rear of the Capitol building loomed large and gray. Outside the library, on the frozen, salt-crusted circular drive, sat the school buses ready to launch.

Blair's laptop screen blinked back and forth between Excel spreadsheets. Suddenly, a cold chill ran down his spine.

★   ★   ★

Deep below the National Security Agency (NSA) offices in Fort Meade, Maryland, a new name arrived for the group to discuss. As the first Super PAC in action, these six people had been meeting as needed for the last five years—long before the moniker was given to the moneyed politicos of the world. The director of the group, her identity kept a confidential secret even to two U.S. presidents, was always on her game. Never a dull minute with her genius. Each action and reaction was carefully reviewed and a unanimous decision of the group was expected.

There were political economic threats well before the Supreme Court heard arguments from Citizen's United, and since a decision was eminent this January, the NSA was tracking them more routinely. In fact, they were working as the sole agency looking at political corruption connected to PACs and the way lobbyists worked the system. It was no secret the government was for sale. It was simply a matter of finding the price—the NSA was prioritizing the price-setters regardless of their party or group affiliation.

Today's discussion was the elimination of a subject who loomed as a threat. A loose cannon diagnosed with a borderline personality and the vindictiveness to create violence, who had worked in Michigan, Illinois, Alaska, and Washington D.C., continued to be unpredictable. At this same meeting, giving another subject protection for the public crucifixion he suffered and the impending threat of further harm would be discussed.

The Super PAC wasn't sure which was going to happen first.

Chapter 2

"**Hey, Parker.** You see Friday's paper about the anti-union crap going on in Lansing and all the PAC money?" barked Tony sitting a couple tables away.

"Yeah, weren't you mixed up in that racket?" asked Chad, who was sitting next to Tony.

Hal chimed in from another table. "Parker was *the* man. Go ahead, tell them what ya can't tell them, Parker. Maybe it'll shut 'em up."

"Come on guys, leave Parker alone," said Mary. "Can't you see he's ready to gin?" Mary was looking over Parker's shoulder at his hand.

"Crap. Again?" exclaimed Sam.

"Come on, guys. You know if I tell you, I'd have to kill you— or someone might kill me," Parker said with a laugh. Parker had stopped talking about his past last year, once everything was put to bed. He had decided there was nothing of value in reliving bad times.

The glass shattering and the loud boom happened simultaneously. Everyone ducked. No one moved except to turn slowly toward the sound, which strangely seemed like it came from the front of the cafe. They saw no one and the street was quiet.

Parker didn't notice the searing pain until seconds later when he attempted to move toward Sam. She looked over and screamed.

"Parker! You're bleeding!"

Without responding, he fell over the table and watched the chaos begin. He heard footsteps and people yelling for help. All he could feel was a burning in his chest and difficulty breathing. *This is it,* he thought. A smile came over his face. All the hard work to finally find a place in life, a rebirth of sorts in favorite places, and he couldn't catch a break. The countless hours of confession, a relentless epiphany of the soul that made for brighter sunrises and deeper sunsets—all disappearing as his breathing got harder. He felt people grab him. Through a strange gray in his vision, he saw Sam holding a towel against his chest.

Sam had been alone for five years before meeting Parker. They'd met at one of Parker's lectures, but didn't see or speak to each other again for six months. Once Parker was settled in his new community of Harbor Springs, they began to notice each other. More importantly, they began to realize the similarities in everything they did and believed in. Sam was one of only a few people who knew of Parker's past. Until now, she thought it was just that—his past.

She softy whispered, "You'll be fine honey. You are not going to die." Then she began to quietly sob as her tears dripped on Parker's cheek. As his eyes began to close, he found comfort in the warm security of her tears. All he could think about was how slow his mind was moving and how refreshing that was; how mindful the moment had become.

Chapter 3

Parker's mind wandered through the years of grief and into serenity as he felt a rolling motion, a sensation of being lifted, and then something cold and solid underneath. It seemed he was floating; he could only make out subtleties of surface and movement. He wasn't sure if his eyes were open or shut, and there were moments when he wanted to smile as he thought of his kids, fishing, and backyard ballgames.

There were voices but no discernible words. They were getting more rapid and forceful. Fishing. The peace of fishing. Suddenly there was heat and pain, and a flash of the abuse. The anger and torment of what was put to rest in some deep synaptic junction far away in the gray resurfaced. The heat left. He was in a yard. Swings, playhouses, trees. Plastic bats swung at white whiffle balls while kids laughed and ran the bases. Giggles while waiting for the next pitch.

The voices were softer … the images faded.

Silence.

Darkness.

★   ★   ★

Blair had left the Michigan Library and was driving east on Jolly Road toward home. The grinding in his gut wouldn't go away. He kept phoning his wife, but she wouldn't answer. He stopped at Dusty's for a bottle of wine and some bread for dinner. Spaghetti was a favorite, and it was a night without kids. *What the hell was happening?* He'd known her for two years; things weren't the same as they were then, but he just kept thinking they'd get better. Every day brought a new twist, and in some sick fashion he was getting addicted to the unknown. *Oh well.* He shook his head and smiled. *Tonight will be okay.*

★   ★   ★

An easy pull of the trigger and it was done. In one fluid motion the revolver slid into the black-leather bag; it was still smoking. No one was around to notice the shooter walk around the corner over to Bay Street and east toward the car. *Schmuck. He was nothing but a coward in Chicago. This took longer to arrange than it should have. Oh well, one more eliminated.*

Chapter 4

The director of the Super PAC took a final accounting of the group's opinions. The decision to eliminate had been given. The protection issue was a continued debate. After the members filed out of the small room, the director closed the door and sat. The room was quiet aside from the buzz in the electronic equipment and florescent lights. She stared at the two names still projected on the computer screen mounted on the windowless wall in front of her. She sat back and put her hands under her chin and wondered what dominos would be next to fall.

★   ★   ★

The Mercedes drove down Mitchell Street to U.S. 31 South. The left turn took a while as traffic slowly turned onto the icy road. The radio played Pink Floyd and the text messages from home talked about dinner. Suddenly a text came in from someone nearby. The car turned back toward Emmet. In the old part of town, where there were historic grocery-store fronts and resale shops, the Benz pulled up the drive.

Into the house and off with the coat.

"I saw you. I know what you did." He looked confident, with

a lit cigarette half out of his mouth that bounced with his lips as he spoke. One eye was closed to guard from the smoke. His head moved up and down as he looked at the sleek figure before him. He smiled and shook his head. Laughing, he looked up. "I can't believe …"

The shot was quick and to the forehead. There wasn't much left of the back of his head. The glove pushed the door open. No one was expected in the home. No one else lived there.

★   ★   ★

Blair read the text over and over. "Just wait till I get home. Life will never be the same." There was always an unpredictability he found exciting. She was exciting. His work was a pain in the ass; research was so boring but necessary. The sauce simmered and the smell of garlic filled the home. Over the granite countertops, through the hall, into the piano room, and down the stairs into the game room, the iconic aromas brought thoughts of candles and checkered tablecloths. A smile came slowly as he anticipated the sex on top of the dinner table once all was consumed. The dessert was always the best part.

★   ★   ★

Parker's mind wandered. He saw tubes and lines on machines, roads, trains, planes, people yelling, people pointing … silence. The last three years of caution, of just trying to be. Now what? The plan was to get to zero and then recreate the dream of bike trips and backpacking. No debts; payments gone. He'd actually reached a mental state of making time to do what he wanted. It was his time. There was a touch he remembered. It was soft. It was on his cheek. He couldn›t tell if it was real. Why is someone calling my name? The last several years came to him. He drifted off.

Chapter 5

The Beginning
Michigan, Illinois, and Washington D.C.—2006-2007

It was a quiet summer day in 2006 when the midnight-blue Chevy Tahoe drove up the long driveway. The white, saltbox house sat on five acres in the farmlands of Ingham County, Michigan, about fifty yards from the road. There were two mature maple trees to the left of the house in front of the pole barn, and a classic weeping willow in the backyard shaded two chairs and a table on hot sunny days. The Tahoe pulled into the parking area that was the basketball court midway up the drive. Two men stepped out and slowly walked toward the house.

Parker was sitting on the front porch he had just finished building the week before. The landscaping was new; the bushes still had tags and the mulch was a dark brown as it had not yet been bleached by the sun. He looked up from the book he was reading to watch the scene unveil before him. The two men were in their thirties, he suspected, both wore sunglasses, and both looked around as they walked one behind the other up the walkway.

"Parker Moore?" the first man to the porch asked. His unbuttoned suit coat was navy blue and he wore a muted red tie. He stopped on the top step just below the deck, set one foot up and leaned forward. The other man stayed behind and kept turning his head as if to survey a crowd that wasn't there.

"Yes. Can I help you?" Parker remained seated but was becoming protective of his domain. He felt himself tense.

"I'm Agent Ramsey and this is Agent Brooks. We'd like to speak with you for a minute, if we could." His manner was easy and he smiled, trying to put Parker at ease. As he spoke, he pulled out an ID so Parker could read it.

"NSA? Wow! I've had to deal with the DEA and FBI before ... What's this about?" Parker's affect eased, and he answered with a smile. He had no idea why they were there but he was flattered that the National Security Agency knew he existed.

During his time as CEO of the Impaired Professional Program for Michigan, he was often visited by the DEA and FBI as they tried to circumvent federal law covering the confidentiality of physicians in the program. The visits would always be professional and cordial, but Parker was held to a strict law of confidentiality. The DEA once sent three agents, including two in very short skirts who looked like they could have walked off the set of a *Miami Vice* episode. They, too, left without the information they sought.

"Well," the agent said, as he looked to his right at the pole barn, took off his sunglasses, and turned his gaze on Parker. "We'd like to discuss a proposition with you. May we come inside?"

Parker was home alone. His wife, Stefanie, had gone to the piano bar in East Lansing with her friends. If it was a normal Saturday, he would have no idea when to expect her home.

"Sure. Can I offer you something to drink?"

"Actually, yes. If you had some coffee, that would be great. We've been in airports all night."

Parker nodded yes, and held the door open for the two agents. Agent Brooks removed his sunglasses as he passed by and nodded at Parker. Parker sat the two men in the living room, facing the large backyard and the rose garden he had planted. The coffee grinder took only a few seconds and within minutes the coffee maker was on. The agents looked around the room. Parker's home office was connected, and they were looking at the plaques, diplomas, and awards on the wall.

"You've been pretty active in your career. How long you been in the Chicago office?" It was the first he'd heard from Agent Brooks.

"Oh, I guess almost two years now." Parker walked around the counter and sat on one of four stools where the kids usually ate.

"We've been following your work through the *Trib* and some of the interviews you've done on WGN. How does that work with you being in Chicago most of the week and not here at home, in Michigan?" Brooks asked.

Parker froze without answering the question. He stared at Brooks and tried to keep a steady, calm affect as he felt the sick, anxious bubbling in his gut. The physical abuse had stopped, but the mood swings and crazy-loud arguments hadn't.

"It's okay. Hard at times, but it's a great career and fits my passion for what I do."

"Which is?" Brooks knew in a moment he was hitting the nerve he sought. They were tired and had a flight to catch that night, so no fooling around with this interview. His orders were clear.

Parker got up to pour the coffee. "Cream? Sugar?"

"No. Black for me," Brooks answered.

"I'll take mine black too," he heard from Ramsey.

"My passion?" asked Parker as he looked at the coffee cups he was carrying to the agents. "It's health care. Always has been and I suspect always will be. I set out to change the world after watching most of my relatives die in hospitals."

"How is it you got involved in the unions, associations, and the lobby side of things?" Brooks wondered.

"Just luck, I guess. I kept getting offers every few years from groups that wanted some new energy and somebody who didn't stop until the job was done." Parker was back on the stool sipping his coffee.

Ramsey stood up, coffee mug in hand, and walked over to the window to look out at the roses. "You've been able to work in a couple states, and we've found you haven't lost a piece of legislation you wanted. We also found you spending a lot of money on legislators. We're not saying you're doing anything wrong. I mean, after all, bar tabs and food aren't illegal."

"Okay, so schmoozing is not good?" said Parker. "I mean, yes, I've found that being active, connected, and offering good arguments for a cause really can work. Money? I don't know where you're going with that."

"Didn't you just have a gathering in Springfield where you dropped about $2,000 in the steakhouse right across from the Capitol?"

Parker looked down and smiled, but was beginning to feel uneasy.

"It was closer to $2,500. And, yes, in fact, it was the largest legislative turnout ever recorded for my group. Only two of the House and Senate members didn't make an appearance. Is that a problem?"

"No," Brooks chimed in as he put his coffee on the living room table in front of the sofa. He turned to look at Parker. "Actually, it's your success that brings us here. Other groups drop thousands; even millions. You? Twenty-five hundred. But, we're still curious about your home life. One of our agents working in Chicago noticed scratches on your forearms when you made an appearance at the Navy Pier. We found out from a colleague of yours that they were from your wife. Is that true?"

Parker was nearly paralyzed. Who in the hell knew about that, and why was it important to a couple of spooks that usually worked anywhere but in public? There was no immediate connection to the money for the legislators and the scratches that resurfaced to the front of his mind. He'd been worried that he'd felt more and more dissociative while essentially living on instinct, but was shocked how suddenly real life felt. He glanced at his forearms before answering, turning them outward so he could look at where her nails dug in that night. Scar tissue remained.

"Mr. Moore?" Ramsey pressed. No one was smiling. "Look, we're actually on your side, but we want to make sure you understand what's going on. We know your wife is cheating on you—a lot. We know she's using your money to buy property elsewhere. We know about the abuse. We also know that instead of leaving, you're ruining your career. We need an inside person. If you help us, we can, perhaps, take care of things for you and allow you to be clear to take care of yourself."

Parker was shaking. He was angry and afraid. He had suspected his wife was having multiple affairs, but he didn't know about the property. *Why the NSA?* This was something out of a Tom Clancy novel. "Okay. I'm really confused. What property?"

"An apartment complex. We don't want to tell you the details, mostly because we don't want you to react in some stupid fashion. We need you. You work with us; we make it all go away. You don't, your life explodes. Are you willing to listen?" Brooks was being sympathetic yet straightforward.

Parker suddenly felt released. He'd been mortified by the physical abuse and driven to the brink of suicide by the mental anguish. The nights he'd locked himself in the kids' rooms when she was on a rampage. The worry that he knew she had her first husband arrested when he finally retaliated. The shame he felt at hiding what he now realized everyone probably knew. That explained why people in town always avoided them as a couple. Why guys would come up and ask if everything was okay. Why all the money he made never seemed to be enough.

Parker had twenty years' experience in the diagnosis and treatment of impaired individuals with alcoholism, mental illness, and personality disorders. He lectured around the country on the subjects and did interventions; he knew he was in an untenable situation with a borderline personality, but he had become the proverbial frog in a pot of water—the frog stayed in the water as it heated up and was eventually boiled to death because the effect of the temperature rising was so subtle. Parker had been having physical symptoms, like heart palpitations. He'd lost interest in his children. He was taking sleeping pills. He suddenly realized his wonderful life was a ruse. A phony. A fake. The trophy, swimsuit-model wife was a demon. The house and all that went with it a Brigadoon. Fear and panic rushed over him. The life he gave up for this. The life he thought was better crumbled before him.

"Mr. Moore, we believe we can help. We know this is hard on you, but we have a reason. Are you willing to listen? Mr. Moore?" Brooks was beside Parker, looking down at him.

"Yes. Yes. What the hell do you want from me?"

"We received reports the governor of Illinois has made threats of holding up legislation for payments to his campaign. We also heard you are the only one getting signatures on your bills. We also know you've had major arguments with the governor's campaign manager and labor staff and that it all went away once you paid money to the campaign of his favorite senator. And last but not least, you're probably going to meet the Democratic candidate who will be running for President of the United States, and he needs to distance himself from what's going on in his home state."

"Wait. Hold on." Parker interrupted. "What the hell is all of this? Why the NSA and why me? Isn't this FBI territory?"

Brooks and Ramsey looked at each other. It was Brooks who answered. "We need a dupe. An inside person. We're a special group working with a group called a Super PAC to root out governmental influence that's become a greater threat than terrorism."

"Super PAC? A political action committee doesn't involve the NSA."

"This one does, Mr. Moore. You know who we are. We hear and see everything. The economy, our public welfare, our entire way of life is on the fringe of disaster because state governments and Washington are based on bribes and pyramid schemes. We have governors trying to sell legislation, political groups putting up candidates simply to increase their already enormous wealth, and unions doing the same thing. The reality is that there are outside influences from other countries doing this. They can't beat us with their militaries. They can't beat us with their technology, so they hit us at our weakest point—political influence.

"The American public is so misled by media and social issues that foreign groups, and some American-based wealth groups, have learned to manipulate world power much like the latest James Bond scenarios. These groups are real, Mr. Moore, and we're signing up as many individuals as we can, through whatever means, to bring down these people."

"A Super PAC? Who's in it?" Parker was smiling in disbelief. Political action committees were all about raising cash for elections and influence.

"Osama bin Laden is not the greatest threat to the American way of life. It is our wealthiest groups who sell us out to the highest bidder. We've been doing secret research through MIT that proves this. A few influential people in our country, some you even know and have worked with, realize the end is near for our way of life if we don't intercede. You are one of many we're taking to task in an attempt to thwart the economic and political apocalypse of our society. Like most, we have something over you, and you have a choice of helping us or falling into the abyss. You agree to work with us and we will take care of you. You don't, and well, most likely the Department of Labor puts you in prison because the groups you defeat want you out of the game. It's no secret hospitals and health-care groups are the fastest growing part of the economy—and you have the perfect opportunity to be our eyes and ears. Trillions of dollars will put people like you away forever. Quite frankly, Parker, you're dead already. Your wife might not kill you but someone else will."

Parker got off the stool and brushed Brooks' shoulder as he walked by him toward the chair next to the sofa. The same chair Parker would sit in late at night before his wife would come downstairs screaming at him for being awake and not in bed with her. He looked at the arms of the chair and felt the anguish of a lost soul. He settled in. The summer day had turned sour. Rain was pelting the windows and the roses were being buffeted in the wind. Most of the petals were gone.

The agents were both standing. Coffee long gone, they waited for Parker.

"What do I do?"

Chapter 6

Parker Moore was a six-five, two-hundred-and-fifty-pound, forty-eight-year-old man who was afraid of nothing–except his wife. He was cool under pressure, whether in a Senate hearing, confronting a violent person, or on a backpacking expedition in grizzly country. Growing up in the Detroit area, he was born of blue-collar roots. He played sports as a kid and had a penchant for a very fast slider that averaged eight strikeouts a game. Through junior high and into high school, he was in the Honor Society, took Latin, physics, and was a geek before it was cool. There was the perception that he could get along with anyone. He was the only kid in school with a briefcase, pocket protector, and a baseball glove. No fights. No drugs.

In spite of the fact his parents understood nothing about college, Parker worked his way through undergrad and graduate school, then taught college and owned his own health-care consulting firm. The calls began. Companies needed a hired gun, and with Parker's physical size and mental agility, he fit the profile. Before he was forty-one, he was worth a million dollars.

Then, the bottom fell out. He and his wife gave up their business for various reasons, including a loss of continuity with each other. The same year, the board of directors he was working for severed his contract after three years and after the board chairwoman indicated in a private meeting that Parker brought out the animal in her. He never gave her that kind of attention, and after a while she got rid of him. Personal issues between Parker and his wife rose to the surface; Parker figured he was becoming more of a depressive and less of a bright star and suddenly he wasn't a great example of executive leadership.

In any case, he continued to teach; tried his hand at owning a sporting goods store; and then found himself back in the lobby, union, and health-care world after two years; however, his marriage of twenty-five years couldn't stand the strain and it deteriorated. The divorce was emotionally hard, but everyone in the family stayed close. The children were the most important issue, so whatever it took, Parker made sure it happened.

Soon after, he met the woman who would become his second wife. Stefanie said her first husband was abusive and a drug addict. But at five nine, one hundred and thirty-four pounds, a perfect size three, and the hair, smile, and sexual demeanor to go with it, he married her and became stepdad to her three kids. Parker moved into their home and immersed himself in her life. In addition to the responsibilities Parker had with his new family, he still had his own three children, and he began a taxing executive job in Chicago that required extensive travel.

The arrangement of working in Chicago was not uncommon for people who lived in Southern Michigan. Jobs were scarce in the Great Lakes State and many people in his hometown worked in Ohio, Indiana, or Illinois. Compared to many, it was actually a luxury for Parker to be home four nights a week. He put over one hundred thousand miles on his car in two years, plus numerous train rides and flights all over the country.

Stefanie felt it was unfair that Parker worked and lived part-time in Chicago. Parker was able to spend time in one of the most exciting cities in the U.S. and she wasn't. He was convinced she was jealous because she worked in a back office opening mail—or so he thought. There was a constant projection that Parker was fooling around. What Parker realized later was the projection was her reality.

It wasn't long before he realized there was something drastically wrong. Her mood swings were the first hint. He gave her the benefit of the doubt. Maybe she was working through the abuse from her first husband, but her anger and the disappearing acts worsened. She socialized with people who took drugs, and she was usually drunk. *Why were drugs okay for her friends but not her ex-husband?* When drunk, she was like Joanne Woodward in *The Three Faces of Eve*, or she'd act like a porn star. The problem was, Parker never knew who would be arriving home or going out with him—and the personality could change in an instant, which is what she had said about her ex. It took a little longer, but Parker eventually realized she was most likely the instigator of the violence.

All conversations and discussions in the house erupted. She liked sex when mad; to the point of demanding Parker rape her.

Parker stayed. Just like everything else he was involved in, he thought he could fix it. Instead, he was rapidly becoming dissociative and confused, which is when the violence started. While on a cruise, after three nights of horrible arguments, he found her flirting with strange men in the bar. When he got her back to their room, she beat the living hell out of him. He'd hold her down until she calmed, then when he would go sit and take a deep breath, she would attack again. The tirade went long into the night; worse than any psychotic patient or criminal he'd ever had to subdue. He wept as he tried to calm her. This was his wife. He knew if he hit her or fought back, he would end up like her first husband–in jail. He could have killed her with one punch. He actually thought about throwing her overboard off the balcony. Instead, he took the beating until he finally ran out of the room and asked for separate sleeping quarters. His arms were bleeding, he had two broken ribs, a broken finger, and was never to be the same.

For the next two years, he experienced much the same. He was afraid of her. One day when she was backing the car out of the garage, she hit him, and then got out of the car to scream at Parker. He knew he was in danger, but worse, he was losing track of what he was doing everywhere else. She would show up at legislative golf outings dressed like a *Sports Illustrated* swimsuit model, so all the legislators loved inviting Parker. One morning, she came to a board meeting and sat in the audience wearing a Victoria's Secret lounging outfit to make a point to the women in the room.

Parker just kept functioning. His trophy wife was charming outside and Linda Blair at home. In fact, he expected her head to turn 360 degrees during the nightly screaming sessions.

Parker's first family had pretty much deserted him; she was so destructive to his children, they stopped visiting. All of his support and social life was gone. He was an automaton functioning on instinct and survival skills. He was making horrible business decisions and had no personality left.

Between his anger and reactions to her anger, the marriage was abusive—and it wasn't only her. If you continue in a violent relationship, then you are a part of it. He never hit or shoved Stefanie, but the vitriol that came out of his mouth scared him. Nothing worked to remove it. Not enough Mass on Sundays. Not enough confessions.

He never would have guessed this is where he would end up. What made the situation desperate was the fact that the health-care world he had devoted thirty-two years of his life to had abandoned him. He had helped write and pass legislation to protect and care for health professionals who had difficulties with drugs, alcohol, mental illnesses, and other circumstances so they could keep their licenses after they recovered. He hadn't told everyone yet what was going on, but those who knew wanted him out. The Machiavellians who wanted the power and prosperity wanted to destroy him.

Stefanie, on the other hand, never had it so good. She had her first husband's house, his child-support payment, Parker's executive income, and a cadre of shallow friends, relatives, and lovers. She knew how to use her looks and Parker was the latest dupe.

The incest in her family and the ridicule she experienced while growing up in her small home town would go away with the more money and influence she could find. She had so much to prove—and in walked Parker. She knew he was the last step to riches. She had to learn about the wealthy side of life—fine wines, four-star hotels, travel, designer clothes—so she could fit in. A bubbling borderline personality created from childhood. Parker used those diagnostic terms with her during countless arguments, and once she realized what he meant, she had to get rid of him. He could ruin her life. She had to ruin him first, though, no matter what.

Chapter 7

Two NSA agents were in his living room, telling him they knew everything. He was as relieved as he was petrified. He would have become Dr. Faustus and made a pact with Mephistopheles if necessary.

The NSA agents described what Parker had to do.

"Besides Illinois, your cover will involve regular trips to D.C. and as much lobby work as you can muster. Gather information and make contact with your handler at least once a week. The locations may be anywhere in the country. Cell phones will never be used unless it's an emergency. People will wonder why you eat lunch on your own; just let them wonder. It will be no different than what you do now."

"How will I be contacted?" Parker was intrigued. He was sitting forward in the chair, listening intently. How long had they been watching him?

"We'll find you. At different events across the country, the agent will be waiting. We also want you to mingle with as many attorneys as possible. They act as the mouthpieces."

"Okay. So I go back to my routine in Chicago. I usually take the train from East Lansing and arrive at Union Station around eleven or twelve. What happens?" Parker didn't think it could be as simple as walking off the train and into an agent's arms.

"Make your way down Adams toward the office. Like I said, we'll find you. In fact, do you know the Rookery Building right behind yours? We'll probably walk you up. After that, when you're in your apartment in Evanston, you'll be in good company." Brooks was talking like Jack Webb in *Dragnet*.

This is obviously a talk he's had with many. "Good company?" Parker asked, perplexed.

"We'll always be around, Parker."

"Got it." Parker wondered how this could work since he roomed with his best friend and COO. Was his wife in on this–from the opposite side? Maybe the whole setup was to get a person on the inside opposite this Super PAC and the NSA.

"Don't worry about your roommate. We won't be that obvious," Ramsey said as if he was reading Parker's mind.

Brooks looked at his watch and motioned Ramsey out the door with a nod.

"We have to run, Parker. Are we good here?" Ramsey was outside and heading to the car; Brooks walked toward the front door. Parker followed, composed and confident.

"If you guys take good care of me, I can deliver on this," Parker said, stopping to look Brooks directly in the eye.

"That's what we're counting on, Parker. That's what we're counting on. We three are going to be very close." Brooks walked out the door, down the stairs, and into the car.

★　★　★

Deep underground, a door closed. Six people sitting around a long conference table started to review the lists. The NSA handled all cyber-intelligence for the United States. NSA dated back to the end of World War Two, and now the agency was engulfed in a new direction involving Homeland Security. The Federal government didn't do much to publicize the NSA, and the agency liked it that way. Parker Moore's name on the list included a strikethrough. It was directly above a few names he would recognize.

Chapter 8

Parker walked off the train at Union Station in Chicago and worked his way through the crowd out onto Adams Street. He headed west toward his office. At LaSalle and Adams stood the Rookery Building. Built by Burnham and Root and completed in 1888, it was the oldest high-rise in Chicago. It still maintained the original Frank Lloyd Wright lobby.

Parker saw Todd Ramsey standing outside the entrance on LaSalle reading a *Chicago Sun Times*. When Ramsey saw Parker, he hesitated to make sure they saw each other, then he turned and walked inside.

"So, Parker, you doing okay with this—after some thought?" Ramsey was headed upstairs with Parker several steps behind him.

"Not much choice, really." Parker loved the open air of the lobby. He always felt, like most people, the architect had the perfect match for buildings and surrounding Nature.

"True. But we might as well make the best of it. We know your nature Parker, so that's why we chose this building." Ramsey was slowing down. Without looking back, he said quietly to Parker, "Head to the restroom. Come out after about five minutes and head into National Exports."

Parker didn't answer back. He walked into the restroom. Needing to use the restroom after a four-hour train ride was routine. When

Parker exited, he made sure it looked like a regular visit to National Exports. No looking around suspiciously or gazing up and down the hall at people before walking in.

"Nice place." Parker was looking at a desk, a laptop, two chairs, a couch, and some plants. No phone. No fax machine. One window looked out at the LaSalle Bank across the street to the north. Shades partially closed. The paint in the room was stark white. No paintings or pictures. "I assume this disappears in minutes?"

"Seconds," answered Ramsey as he began to place Parker's equipment on the desk. "Here's your pin mic. Small and simple. Just remember, when on, we hear everything." Ramsey smiled. "Please, please remember that."

"Okay." Parker was sitting in a wooden side chair with his hands on his knees. He was somewhat nervous but strangely confident.

"Just go about your day. We've got your cell and work phones in our system, and we can track you anywhere with this. Keep it with your Day-Timer." Ramsey looked at Parker's appointment book. They knew Parker wasn't a fan of personal technology and preferred a pen over a smart phone or Palm Pilot.

"Who listens?"

"Us. That's all you need to know."

"If I get into trouble?"

"We're always close, Parker."

"You know, there's already been months of bullshit?" Parker was sitting as he was before.

Ramsey was across from him, stretched out on the couch with his legs crossed at the ankles.

"We know. Now we can get what you still have to do."

"Okay," Parker said, standing with a big sigh. "Will you always be here when I need something?"

"No. Just when you come into town. Before you leave, I'll find you."

"Thanks, Ramsey," Parker said without emotion.

"See ya, Parker. Business as usual." Ramsey had his hands folded behind his head.

Parker nodded and walked out the door.

Chapter 9

"Hey, Carlos. Good weekend?" Parker walked by the guard at the front desk.

"Great, Mr. Moore. You?"

"Interesting." Parker smiled as he waited at the bank of elevators with about twenty other people. He was holding his briefcase with two hands in front of him, and he was very aware of his wire.

An elevator opened to his left. Parker got in with six other people dressed as he was–suit, tie, and computer briefcase. Most were checking their BlackBerrys. No one talked.

When the elevator finally reached the 22nd floor, he was the only person left on the elevator. He stepped out and waited momentarily. The door closed behind him, and he turned and looked at the gray doors of the vault he had just exited. His briefcase was still held by both hands in front of him. Finally, he turned to his right and walked down the long hallway to his office. There were no other offices on the floor since it was being renovated. Some plaster dust lay before him on the tan carpet. Three lights hung as sconces on the walls.

"Here I go, Mr. Ramsey. I sure hope this works out for you *and* me," Parker said quietly as he opened the door.

"Parker. Put your briefcase in your office and then follow me." It was Cindy, his staff labor attorney. She was with him in

Michigan as well. "You have to give a speech to the Cook County Commissioners about the state of public health around Cook County. Here. Read this."

Cindy followed Parker to his office and placed a legal pad in front of him as he bent down to put his briefcase next to his desk. The window shades were open, as always. Except for two feet on each side of the window, Parker had eighteen feet of glass to look eastward into Chicago's Loop. His desk always faced the window since Parker didn't like anyone having to talk over a desk. When someone entered to meet with him, they either sat on the sofa, a side chair, or at the small conference table and chairs near the door. The north windows stretched twenty feet and looked directly into the executive offices of LaSalle Bank across Adams. Below the windows in front of his desk looking east was Clark Street. He had to rise over the desk and look down, but often had his window open so the noise of the day came up and allowed him to use his imagination of the street scene.

"What the hell, Cindy?" He was already on his way back out of the office with Cindy tugging at his arm.

"We've got a contract due and you're setting the tone for our negotiations–publicly!"

"Isn't that a little shady, putting them on the defensive already? They're going to see right through that."

"Tough shit."

"Yeah. Easy for you to say. I'll get the phone call from John Stroger. Not you." Parker smiled. He'd completely forgotten about the wire. "Hell, they already named the new hospital after him. I think he'll believe he can overpower me."

Parker and Cindy headed into an elevator and then back outside onto Clark Street, walking north toward the County Building.

Chapter 10

"Thank you for the budget update. Now we have some public information time. Our first speaker is Mr. Parker Moore— one of our local health-care union executives. Mr. Moore, you have five minutes."

John Stroger, president of the Cook County Board, was a larger man than his reputation–and that was huge. His insight into health care and public health didn't get much past his waistline, but he was liked and respected by many, including Parker. However, Stroger's administration was in turmoil and scandals were commonplace. The press beat him up continually.

"Thank you, President Stroger." Parker was at the podium. There were at least one hundred people crammed into the chamber, as always. People mulled about and talked in hushed tones. There was rarely total quiet, unless John Stroger was speaking.

Parker gave a five-minute speech about the difficulties within the Cook County schools concerning immunizations and the general health of the students. It made Stroger look bad in the eyes of the parents in the room.

"Mr. Moore," John Stroger started as he stared at Parker, "your inference that staffing is an issue to continue our mandates is more than an inference. Your group's contract is up soon, isn't it?"

"Yes, sir." Parker quickly glared at Cindy who was standing next to him. "Here it comes," Parker whispered under his breath as his teeth still showed a smile.

"Very well. I will call you." John Stroger spoke sternly and without waiver. His voice deepened when he said *you*.

"I'll look forward to that, sir." Parker nodded and left the podium with Cindy in tow.

They walked past people standing, people sitting on the floor, people in business suits having private conversations, a few homeless folks watching the show, and anybody else who could squeeze inside the room.

"Geez, Cindy. I told you."

"Yes, Parker, but you usually close things quickly and this one was lingering. Have you been okay? "

"Well, it won't be lingering long. Stroger will be on the phone by the time I get back into the office." Parker wasn't upset; in fact, he was proud of Cindy. He was more girding for battle than admonishing her for her work. He didn't ignore her question. He just didn't respond.

They were walking south on Clark toward Adams.

"Really, Parker, what's up lately? It's like you're in a trance." Cindy was trying to keep up with Parker's long strides amid throngs of people.

"Nothing's up. It's been hard at home working here. Like two worlds. Sometimes it catches up with me. Hey, let's duck into Stan's office for a minute and tell him what we just did."

Stan Levinson was the chief partner in the crack labor firm Parker's union group used when Cindy needed some punch. They entered his building off of West Monroe and waited for the private elevator to the firm's office.

"Let's get Stan in on this, since you're going to be busy with negotiations in two places. He knows Stroger better than anyone." Parker stood next to Cindy as they both watched the old-fashioned elevator lights above the doors as the chime marked each floor passed by the descending elevator.

Once inside, it was a direct flight to the top. Off the elevator,

Parker and Cindy asked for Stan and were ushered into the side conference room.

"Coffee or water?" asked Pam, the receptionist.

"Coffee for me. Black," Parker said as he sat in the comfortable pub-style conference chairs.

"Nothing for me. Thanks," said Cindy.

Before Pam left for the coffee, Stan was already coming in to sit down with a legal pad that had several pages flipped over the binding.

"Don't tell me. You're here because of the speech you just gave to the commissioners?" Stan said. His white, striped shirt was rolled up at the sleeves and his red-paisley tie was loosened at the collar.

"Already?" Parker asked.

"You weren't out of the room yet, Moore. Sheesh! Next time before negotiations, be subtle with your words and timing." Stan was sitting straight. Both hands on the table held the yellow legal pad. "His people said your push in public won't get to a quick solution."

"Okay," Parker said quietly.

Cindy started to speak, but Parker grabbed her wrist and held her back.

"How public you want to take this, Parker? We'll do whatever you want, but it might get ugly."

"Okay." Parker was biding his time while searching for an answer.

Silence. Pam walked in with Parker's coffee.

"Thanks, Pam. Can you make sure we're not disturbed? Thanks." Stan wasn't going to let Parker leave without some direction, now that Stroger was upset.

Silence.

"You don't need this kind of stress, Parker. The governor's on your butt. Your board's on your butt. God only knows what other stress is going on in your life … Stroger will make your life miserable." Stan was sitting back in his chair. The legal pad was on the table.

Parker contemplated his wire. He contemplated his new mission and how it would all play out. His contract would be up next year, and he was already wondering what would happen. No matter the legislation passed, contracts won and signed, or positive press he received, nothing erased his home life. Nothing erased the turmoil.

"Let's give Stroger a few days to stew; then, I'll call him. I'll apologize for taking him to task in public and not waiting to work through issues at the negotiating table. And, I will point out the great responses we're getting from the governor and the public, and we would just like to make him a part of that. It would be the most positive press he's received in the last year. In the long run, he settles a contract early, with money he knows he's already earmarked, and looks good to the schools, parents, and the press."

"Good deal. I can live with that," Stan said looking at Cindy.

"That's it? You think it will end there?" Cindy asked, flabbergasted at such an easy way out.

"That's it." Parker looked at Stan. "Thanks for the coffee, Stan."

"Any time, Parker. Cindy." Stan stood and opened the door.

Stan reached out and grabbed Parker by the arm while Cindy continued toward the elevator.

"Parker, it's too easy for you. Don't get too complacent. This is the big top. Watch your back." He looked directly in Parker's eyes. He wasn't smiling. "This town eats people like you for a snack."

"Sure, Stan. Thanks." Parker left.

Cindy and Parker made their way out onto Monroe, left on Clark, and back to the office. Cindy didn't say a word. Parker wondered if it would always be this easy.

Chapter 11

Parker was working in Chicago four days a week but only three nights. He always spent a weekend with Stefanie and her kids in Chicago every other month, so he could work in peace during the week, and Stefanie would seem to calm down for a few days. While in Chicago, he and best friend and COO, Dick Hart, shared an apartment in Evanston. The train station was a half mile away from the apartment, and on days they used their cars, Lakeshore Drive was the perfect entry to downtown.

"Hell of a day with the County Board?" Dick said as the two walked toward the Ogilvie Transportation Center on Madison across the canal.

"I guess."

"Easy for you, isn't it?" Dick was looking sideways at Parker. Both were carrying their briefcases like thousands of others headed to the trains at six-thirty in the evening.

"Too easy." Parker wasn't worried at all about the NSA and the Super PAC finding out about business as usual in Illinois, but he was worried he and Dick couldn't have a normal conversation anymore. He was told he could take off the wire in Evanston, but that would be a while. Then it occurred to him that maybe it was a good thing he had it on around town before he got behind locked doors.

"That's why you get paid the big bucks. I could never just walk into a group like that unprepared and pull that off." Dick was the first one through the revolving door as he spoke.

As Parker walked through the doors, he noticed a man in jeans and a navy blue jacket standing quietly amongst the crowd. It was a quick glance, but he noticed the man watching him. Parker and Dick walked up the stairs and into the bar on the left before reaching the train area. The giant board overhead told them they had forty-five minutes to wait. Dick often liked a Budweiser before they took the train home.

"Two." Dick got the attention of the bartender. No stools open, so both men stood.

"You know, it's amazing the amount of people that pass through here every day without skipping a beat. Like ants in the nest doing the same thing over and over, day in and day out for years." Parker took the beer from Dick and took a long swig. The man was gone.

"It's what people do, Parker. Without them doing this, we're outta work." Dick was gazing at the crowded stairs and people at the bottom waiting in line all the way to the revolving doors at the front of the building.

"All this for a lousy two-week vacation?"

"What else do they know?"

"How about a different life?"

"Parker, you *should* have a perfect life. You have amazing children. Stefanie's kids love you. You have a great home, work in a great city, and are only here three nights. Are her looks worth it?"

"What's that supposed to mean?" Parker looked indignant. He'd never had a cross word with his friend and confidante, but he felt defensive.

"Come on, Parker. Every time you're with her or on the phone you're like a robot, afraid to talk or make a move unless she pushes the right button." Dick was drinking the last of his beer.

Parker had been convinced this was his lot in life. Being the first one divorced in his Catholic family, he had never dealt with the guilt. He was going to make this marriage work—no matter what. It would just take time.

"It is what it is. That's all I'll say." Parker drank the last of his beer and looked in the mirror behind the bar. The blue jeans and navy jacket was standing behind him in the bar drinking with a woman.

"I'm just saying people are starting to notice. I'll keep doing what I can, but eventually doing things like getting up in front of hundreds of people and spontaneously speaking is going to get more and more difficult." Dick took Parker's bottle, then reached between two people to set the empties on the bar. "Parker, I got faith in you. Just keep your head." Dick grabbed Parker's left shoulder with his right hand and rocked him back and forth as he smiled.

"Thanks, Dick. You're right on all sides. I'm just taking it day by day right now."

They walked toward the bank of glass doors. Parker noticed the man and woman behind him in the reflection as they walked through to the trains.

★   ★   ★

Stefanie spent the next weekend with Parker and her three children in Chicago. They visited the Field Museum and the King Tut exhibit. Tickets were hard to get and expensive, but as usual she used the money Parker sent home to pay for everything. They ate at four-star restaurants, shopped on Michigan Avenue, and had the time of their lives.

The following Monday, Parker's fourteen-year-old son visited him during the week as it was summer vacation. They spent most of their time playing cards and exploring downtown in between Parker's meetings and other tasks. One afternoon, they decided to visit the Orvis shop just off Michigan Avenue.

"Look at these polo shirts. I can get three for half price!" Parker exclaimed to Nelson.

Parker's size didn't always allow him to shop the average discount stores. There was rarely anything that fit him, so this find was extraordinary. Excited, Parker bought the shirts and called her.

"Honey, you won't believe what I found. Three shirts at Orvis for half price, and they fit!"

There was a long silence. "How much?" was the stern response.

"Ugh, fifty dollars. Usually my shirts cost that much for just one." Parker was hedging his excitement. He could feel the timidity enter his body. After an executive day of major responsibilities, he couldn't believe he was once again cowering on the phone.

"What the fuck business have you got buying three shirts?"

A tirade ensued.

Parker listened and apologized to her while standing amongst a throng of shoppers walking on the beautiful, warm, afternoon by the Water Tower. As much as Parker kept smiling and trying to joke with different facial gestures, Nelson knew what his father was experiencing as he saw the excitement bleed from his dad's face.

Parker couldn't stop thinking about Dick's comments the week before.

Chapter 12

Dick Hart was one of the few who witnessed the abuse. He did not know of Parker's involvement with the NSA. The only thing Dick knew was that Parker had turned into a nut case and he had to bail out Parker by making excuses for his friend's behavior. Explain why Parker acted a certain way. Why the depression was related to job stress, and why Parker never made enough money to keep his wife happy. Everyone looked the other way publicly because Parker got whatever it was they wanted. Legislative influence and union contract victories. Hospitals across the country saw him as a threat, but the people getting salary hikes and their names in the paper loved the attention. They had no idea what was going on.

"The Governor's Office called yesterday." Dick and Parker were walking north on Clark.

It was a Monday, the week after Nelson's visit. Parker and Dick drove into Chicago together this particular week since they had to attend several of the same meetings. They would park the car below the loop, on Clark south of Roosevelt in the dirt lots. Dick didn't like to spend a dime and Parker liked the walk.

"Yeah. Now what?" Was Parker's response.

The July morning sun was hot. The crowds of people didn't begin until they hit Jackson Avenue. Both were dressed in polo shirts for an office day.

"He wants you at a press conference down at the Navy Pier."

"We just did one there." Parker remembered the conversation with Brooks and Ramsey. *How long have they been watching me?*

"This is about legislation he wants your help with, so good union folks can be more successful in the private sector."

"Translated means let the private sector pay for everything and let the public sector employees suffer. He'll get good press, but underneath this is going to blow up."

Parker and Dick crossed under the EL near the LaSalle Station. Parker looked up and saw a woman watching them. She was dressed in a white tank top and short tan shorts. Her blonde hair flowed over her shoulders as if it were placed by a hair dresser. She kept eye contact with Parker and didn't seem shy about it as she leaned on the metal railing.

"Hey, Dick, I gotta make a visit over at the Labor Board in the Rookery. I'll see you later. You want me to bring you something from Starbucks?" Parker stopped in front of the entrance to their building on Clark.

"No. I can make my own coffee. No coffee is worth half a paycheck." Dick smiled, shook his head, and walked through the revolving door into the office building.

Parker walked around the corner and headed west on Adams. He took a look behind him through the Starbucks' windows back toward Clark. The woman was walking into the Starbucks through the Clark Street door. She looked away. *Why avert the glance now?* he wondered.

He found himself picking up his pace as he neared the Rookery Building, and decided to enter the Brooks Brothers store off Adams to cut through into the main lobby. As he opened the door, he saw her walk out of Starbucks through the Adams Street door.

Once inside, he ran upstairs and headed for National Exports. He opened the door and there sat Ramsey. Parker dropped his briefcase and closed the door quickly.

"Who the hell have you got following me? You said I wouldn't be alone, but I didn't realize …" Parker was standing over Ramsey with his hands on the desk top not realizing how fast he was talking and how out of breath he was. Ramsey cut him off in mid sentence.

"Wait. Wait! We don't have anyone following you, Moore." Ramsey came out from behind the desk; his affect calm but serious. "We've been following your phone and your Day-Timer. We don't need to tail you like some 1950's movie." Ramsey sat down in one of the side chairs. He motioned Parker to sit on the couch. He leaned forward and asked Parker in a calm, even voice, "Now, who are you seeing?"

Parker took a deep breath and gathered his thoughts.

"Last week there was a guy, then the same guy with a woman at Ogilvie, and today the same woman from Jackson to here. I assume she saw me go into Brooks Brothers." Parker felt himself getting angry. "So, how confidential am I to this Super PAC?"

"Very."

"I have to be with the governor again today, at the Pier. Something about making a pitch to union folks and health-care professionals. Do I prompt him or just let him talk?"

"Let him talk."

"No word out there I'm working with you?" Parker went back to the people he thought were following him.

"None."

"You're not making me feel secure here, Ramsey. Nothing to add?"

"No."

Ramsey just sat with his folded hands resting on his knees as he looked at Parker.

"Parker, you'll get comfortable. Maybe they're not really following you?" Ramsey sat back and took a breath, separating his hands and clasping them behind his head.

"Have you checked everyone out around me?" Parker persisted. He got up and paced as his left hand rubbed the back of his head. His right arm hung at his side with his fist clenched. He stopped at the window. The shades were partially shut.

"Yes, we've checked everyone out, including your new Labor Executive, Pete. Not everybody has a clean past, but with the business you're in we didn't expect a clean slate. There are no discernible threats."

"Okay. Give me the wire." Parker let Ramsey fix him up and check the equipment.

★   ★   ★

She left Brooks Brothers when she couldn't see him inside and didn't see him anywhere in the lobby of the Rookery. She had waited long enough and knew where he worked, parked, and stayed in Evanston; she wasn't worried about picking him up again. She punched a number into her Blackberry.

★   ★   ★

"There you go, Parker. Just do your thing, and don't worry. You'll get used to this gig. From what I hear, you handle people and crowds like a pro. Good luck with the governor." Ramsey shook Parker's hand.

Parker nodded and walked into the hallway. He didn't look around and made sure he went out the back entrance which opened into the alley between the Rookery and his office building. He saw no one except the usual cleaning and cooking crews outside smoking.

Chapter 13

"**Parker, the** Governor's Office has called three times this morning. They're not being nice anymore." Brenda handed Parker three message slips as he walked in the office.

"Moore, call the goddamn governor, will ya?" Pete yelled from his office, laughing.

Parker poked his head in.

"You don't like him, do you?"

"I voted for him because he's a Democrat. Do I like him? No. Do I trust him? No. But that's my job. By the way, when can we meet about the University of Chicago contract?" Pete had turned from his desk, still sitting in his chair. His Italian looks and demeanor shined brighter than his impeccable suit.

None of the staff had their desks in front of them, facing the doorway of their offices. They liked Parker's openness and copied it. Pete was the last to make the move. Having been in the union business for over twenty years in Chicago, he didn't like his back to any door.

"Tomorrow. I'll make time. I have a call from their attorney for a meet and greet, and I want to have it before we start negotiations so I'm not party to any meeting without the membership. Thanks, Pete." Parker continued down the hall to his office.

★   ★   ★

She was standing on the east side of Dearborn Street looking up past the Post Office building and into Parker's office window. She'd found he never pulled the shades; the morning sun shined brightly on him as he talked on the phone.

★   ★   ★

"Yes, Governor. I will be there. I promise. Yes." Parker was checking e-mails as he talked on the phone.

"Moore, we gotta have ya. The press has been on me, and we need support on TV today. You'll be front and center with me, along with the Teamsters, AFSCME, and the SEIU. Oh, and we need you in Springfield next week for a meeting with our labor staff. Seems you've been stirring the pot a little."

"Just doing my job, sir. What day next week?"

"Not sure. I'll have someone call you. See you at two, Moore." The governor hung up.

Parker put the phone down on the cradle and continued deleting e-mails. Most were continuous streams of the same notes from one to fifty or more people. Once he read a new note he'd only keep the original e-mail in the string. His memory kept track of the others. Parker's three to four hundred daily e-mails were usually gone by the end of the day, along with his phone messages. His days were so spontaneous, if he fell behind one day, it could take a month to catch up.

He scrolled down. Delete. Delete. He saw one that showed up as being previously read. He sat back and wondered how that would have happened. He never worked on e-mails at home. He always tried to maintain a separation between home and work.

As he finished the first go-round through the his e-mails, he looked up at the bright-orange sculpture by the post office on Dearborn Street made famous in *Ferris Bueller's Day Off*. His kids would come to the office and look out the window before they did anything else. Parker smiled.

There she was. Tank top and short tan shorts with blonde hair. She was wearing sunglasses and looking directly at his office window. Parker tried not to react or do anything sudden. He turned back to his computer screen and glanced her way once in a while, careful not to move his head.

She brought her phone up to her ear, and after a few minutes she walked to the corner of Adams and Dearborn. She bent over and talked to someone in a midnight-blue Ford Crown Victoria.

Parker looked behind him to make sure no one could hear his soft tones.

"Ramsey, if you're the one listening, I'm telling you, someone is following and watching me. She's about five foot ten, blonde, wearing a white tank top and tan shorts. I guess she wants to look like someone slumming down here from upper Michigan Avenue."

Parker actually caught himself waiting for a reply.

"What the hell am I doing?" he said softy to himself. "Just do your job, Parker."

"Have you finally lost it?" Dick Hart walked into Parker's office and sat on the couch. "Who you talking to?"

"Me."

"You all set today with the governor?"

"Yes. Hey, can you come with me?" Parker turned toward Dick and sounded needy.

"Sorry, Parker, the Foundation's coming in, and you know how they are."

"All right. No problem. How about next week in Springfield?"

"Sure. Depending on the day. What the hell's with you?" Dick leaned forward a little.

"Just tired of always being alone on the road. Maybe we can take the train and make a day out of it." Parker was smiling as he hid some apprehension.

"Like I said, Parker, we'll see." Dick changed the subject. "The attorney from the University of Illinois-Chicago is asking for you to be at breakfast tomorrow. What's his name? Ben?"

"Okay. I'll call him. You know, he's such a nice guy and always has me over to the Standard Club, but I know it's only to keep ahead of us and get information. These attorneys really feed the system from all angles."

Parker picked up the phone and glanced out the window. She was gone.

Chapter 14

Parker walked to the Navy Pier and looked for the governor's staff to direct him. They pointed toward the back; he made his way to the ballroom at the end of the Pier. He walked outside and saw the crowds of tourists eating at the outdoor restaurants, standing in line for the Ferris wheel, and getting in and out of the sight-seeing boats. He walked with his hands in the pockets of his navy blue sport coat. He had on a white dress shirt and tie. He always kept a change of clothes and two sport coats at the office for spontaneous occasions such as this.

As he perused the scene, he noticed the woman paralleling him inside. The windows allowed tourists to view the outside in bad weather. She was in the hallway to his left.

"Parker Moore?" He looked forward. Two men wearing jeans and navy jackets stood in front of him.

"Yes?" Parker didn't move his hands or act alarmed.

"The governor would like a word with you before he speaks. Could you please follow us?"

The men were shorter than Parker, but bulky. They obviously were the governor's security. The three men walked inside near the parking garage entrance about halfway down the pier where three blue GMC Suburbans waited. The windows were blacked out so Parker couldn't see inside.

The two men pointed to the middle vehicle and the back door opened. Parker did not recognize the older man sitting in the middle seat Parker climbed in as directed.

"Mr. Moore," said the man as he looked directly at Parker. "It's a pleasure to meet you in person. We'll skip the formalities. I'm here to tell you that we know everything about you. We will be needing some cooperation from your political action committee and expect positive press over the next several months, especially as we get closer to the election. There are big plans afoot and you have been—what would be the appropriate way to say it for this setting? Making waves."

The man was dressed in a very expensive suit and took great care in how he sat. He brushed lint off his knees while lecturing Parker.

"Sir, I have no idea who you are or what this is. Is it a shakedown?" Parker wasn't backing off. He felt confident about his wire.

"I assure you, this is no shakedown. The county and the governor have their agenda. You will not muck it up. We've survived for years doing business a certain way, and you coming from out of town need to understand our seriousness. Now, if you'll forgive me." The man nodded to the men in the front seat.

Before Parker could respond, the door was opened and a man firmly grabbed Parker's right elbow. He did not pull, but the message was clear. Parker was to get out.

"Thank you for the …" The door was shut and the SUVs began to drive away. "Shit. Yeah, thanks for the shit." Parker was standing alone. So he thought.

He turned around to head out the south entrance, back to the main outside walkway. He saw the blonde standing against a pillar. One leg back behind her as her left foot rested on the pillar. The other angled straight out in front, making for a long, sleek figure. She was looking at him over a pair of sunglasses perched on her nose. Once Parker stopped walking, she pushed the glasses up and walked outside in front of him. He got to the glass door as it was shutting only to see her blend into the crowd.

Chapter 15

Parker waited with about fifteen people in the Festival Hall. He kept a head count of the VIPs. He wanted to write about the press conference in his board report, so he took careful mental notes. It was past 3:00 p.m.; as usual the governor was late. The reporters and their television cameras were lined up. People leaned on various equipment boxes, sat on the floor, on benches, played with their phones and BlackBerrys, anything to pass the boredom. Parker sat quietly in a chair to the side of the riser. Many were jockeying for position on the riser to be closest to the governor. Since Parker was always the tallest, it didn't matter to him. The cameras always picked him up.

A group of Chicago police officers and Illinois state troopers walked in with the governor. He waved as the people clapped. He shook hands with Parker and everyone on the riser. Parker got up and stood in the middle to the rear.

"Moore? Parker? Come down here and stand." The governor talked over the applause and waved him down. Two men moved to the right, one smiled at the audience and the other sneered at Parker.

"Ladies and gentlemen, thank you for being here today. I would like to talk about a series of legislative initiatives now making its way through the State House. We believe these bills will expand the ability of those in need of health care to receive health care. Expansion of insurance benefits, improved staffing in our hospitals, and scholarships for an increase in health-care professionals in this state."

Everyone applauded. Parker smiled. Everything the governor said was only partially true. His public sector health-care system was a mess, and he wasn't going to do anything about it. The initiatives concerned expansion of the private sector. Poor facilities, mandatory overtime, and no payments for Medicaid care would continue to haunt the public.

Parker smiled as the governor droned on. He scanned the audience and the press. Miss Tan Shorts was standing to the side, talking discreetly with one of the governor's aides. They looked straight ahead while conversing. There were no other people around them to disguise the discussion.

The governor finished and refused to take any questions. Various staff and police stepped between him and the press. He turned to Parker and shook his hand with cameras flashing.

"Springfield. My office, next Wednesday. We'll have a chat." The governor never stopped smiling and talked through his teeth.

Parker smiled. After the governor dropped his hand, Parker left the riser and walked through the crowd and outside. He stopped to look down at the harbor on Lake Michigan; his hands were back in his jacket pockets. He looked around and didn't see the woman. He lowered his head and turned west toward his office. Kids screamed, kids laughed, parents called, couples ate ice cream, tourists clamored for tables at outside bars and cafes. Parker just kept walking.

His phone rang.

"Yes?"

"Parker, I got the message you returned my call." It was Ben Flarrety the attorney representing Illinois-Chicago. "The Standard Club tomorrow at nine. See you there, Parker."

"See ya, Ben." Parker folded his phone and kept walking.

After a period of quiescence, all of a sudden everyone wanted Parker. He wondered about the NSA and the Super PAC. *What was it they really wanted and who were they after? The attorney calls, the attention from the Cook County commissioners, and the governor. It all seemed coincidental to the visit by Brooks and Ramsey, and eerie that everyone who wanted me around has suddenly come calling.*

He kept walking. Past Michigan Avenue.

There was a way of doing politics in Illinois and no one was ashamed of the money. Everyone made out. As executive director, Parker oversaw the PACs of his association and union. He signed all the checks and reviewed the accounting. What was interesting was how much money passed into campaigns even with limits set by the state and federal governments. His Chief Financial Officer and PAC Chair were very conservative, so rules were followed closely. Parker learned after a year and a half around Chicago and Springfield, his group may have been the only one following the rules.

He kept walking. On to State Street, past Marshall Field's.

The attorneys acted as the mouthpieces and bag men. They lobbied without registering as lobbyists. They put people together in a consultative method for causes and groups to have the right audience. When Parker was involved in some of those meetings as an invitee, he was always cognizant of the positioning for power while talking around subjects and never really laying out a point of view. He was hired because he wasn't afraid of the public eye or to speak his constituents' views—but Parker worried he could become the fall guy.

He kept walking. Past the Italian Village on Monroe.

There she was, getting out of the blue Crown Vic at Monroe and Clark in front of him. She acted nonchalant.

"I've had enough of this shit," Parker said softly to himself. He walked directly at her.

Chapter 16

"Can I help you?" Parker shouted as he walked across Clark to the west side of the street.

Parker was walking quickly and obviously angry. The woman didn't seem to know what to do at first. Then she began to run.

"Kiss my ass!" Parker yelled as she disappeared down Monroe.

He turned south on Clark and walked the last block to Adams toward his building. Once inside, he stopped and turned. He waited. She never showed.

By the bank of elevators, he saw Dick.

"How'd it go? You looked good on TV, Parker." Dick was staring at the door in front of him holding a sandwich bag from Potbelly's around the corner.

"You know. Bullshit. He put me in front to keep me quiet. He wants a conference next week on Wednesday. Can you go?" Parker stared at the same door.

"Can't do Wednesday. You do the PAC down there that day, don't you?" The door opened.

Parker walked inside with Dick before answering.

"Yes. How did he know that?"

Neither man said a word the rest of the ride up.

★ ★ ★

She looked at the five men of the Super PAC seated at the small table. They were reading reports.

"What's this in Illinois?" said a man wearing a dark blue suit and shiny, powder blue tie. "The other five states seem to be going smoothly."

"We've got a pickup on something between the governor's office, Cook County, and somebody with lots of money." The leader of the group and the only female, had her glasses down on her nose and was talking as she read.

"Pickup? How?" inquired another gent at the table.

"We have the wire and phone taps. But it was the wire. The FBI is doing some checking as well. We have to keep our distance from them because if we don't, everything we're working on will end up in the public eye." She stopped reading and looked around the room. Everyone was nodding.

★ ★ ★

Stefanie packed up the kids and went to Florida. She did not tell Parker.

★ ★ ★

That evening, after the walk to the car and drive up Lake Shore Drive to their apartment, Dick and Parker watched old *Seinfeld* reruns as they made dinner. Parker had been trying to reach Stefanie all day without success. He sat with the phone to his ear.

Finally an answer.

"Hello?" Her speech was slurred.

"Where are you?" Parker waved to Dick as he went outside and into the courtyard below. Parker didn't want Dick to hear the conversation.

"Orlando!"

"Where are the kids?"

"In the hotel room."

"Alone?"

"Sure. Why?"

"They're not old enough to be alone in a hotel room in Orlando. Where are you?"

"Out with the girls."

She took the phone away from her mouth and Parker heard her yell, "Where are we?" Then she spoke into the phone, "They can't hear me." The crowd in the background was loud.

"How far away from the hotel are you?" Parker felt anger welling up inside of him. He paced.

"I don't know."

"Please, think about what you're doing. Please, go back to the kids."

"Fuck you." The phone went dead.

Parker tried calling back. Nothing. Again and again. Nothing. He sat on a bench and tried to regain his composure. He walked back upstairs and into the apartment.

"Everything okay?" Dick was sitting at the table. Two plates of steaming spaghetti gave off an enticing aroma.

"Yeah. Peachy." Parker sat down and quietly ate while Dick laughed at the "Yada yada yada" episode.

Chapter 17

The train was actually on time. Dick stood against the wall working a Sudoku. Parker walked up and down the wooded walkway next to the train tracks. It was 7:00 a.m. and he knew by the end of the day he'd have a better handle on two major contracts at the University of Illinois-Chicago and the University of Chicago. He also knew when he got home Thursday night all hell would break loose.

He wasn't sure how he was being watched in Evanston, but after the woman in the tan shorts, the meeting with the mystery man in the governor's Suburban, and figuring out what next Wednesday was going to bring in Springfield, Parker was ready to explode. *What brought all of this on?*

He paced.

The train whistle sounded just north of the station where the train came through downtown Evanston. He and Dick called this Metra the Wall Street Train. All the wealthy executives, lawyers, and finance people rode it in from the north suburbs. The *Wall Street Journal* was the newspaper of choice. He and Dick usually opted for the *Sun Times* sports section; although Parker routinely read *Crain's Business*, *The Tribune*, and the *Wall Street Journal* to be up on everything. But he never missed the *Sun's* sports.

"Parker, come on." Dick was looking down the walkway at Parker who was gazing into the early sun with his eyes shut.

The only way Parker survived his marriage was by getting a constant interlude with the outdoors. If meetings became mundane, or days became chaotic, he would walk for miles. In less than a year and a half, he'd resoled his wingtips twice. On bad days, he'd head to the Art Institute of Chicago to sit and stare at the Impressionists works. He'd imagine standing at an easel in some countryside setting of France with nothing but the sky and the scenery. Closing his eyes would ease the abuse and carry him into another century, away from the insanity he was beginning to feel. Life as an executive added to the stress, but in reality, it was easier than being at home.

"Parker! What the hell, man? Come on!"

The train was at the station and the doors open. Parker hadn't moved. He turned and ran for the door Dick was standing in. The conductor was waving at him. As soon as Parker stepped inside, the door closed, and the train was off.

"Get your shit together, Parker. You've got a big breakfast meeting today." Dick ushered Parker to two empty seats facing the aisle near the door of the train.

"I got it, Dick. It's going to be a good day." Parker sat and watched the back of homes, warehouses, and alleys glide by.

The train rides held a blessing and a curse for Parker. In the morning, there was always the excitement of the day ahead. At night, after a twelve-hour workday, Parker would try to have regular conversations with Stefanie. Most often he just listened to her tirades. Then, before bed, the calls would be about forgiveness and love. Every day was a roller coaster of emotions. The worst nights were when he couldn't reach her. He'd get so angry, then relieved once they connected. At that point, Parker Moore wasn't sure what was happening to him.

Ogilvie Station came into view and the sun disappeared as the train entered the cavernous stop. Parker and Dick stood like robots waiting to get off and begin the trek to the office, just like the other thousands of robots.

"You going to talk to Pete today?" Dick asked as they walked down Madison.

"Yes. I think he's doing okay, but the members are getting antsy. He's used to being a Teamster. Never doing health care, we need to keep mentoring him. He's a good negotiator; they'll figure that out."

Parker kept track of everything in his head and could retrieve whatever he needed at a moment's notice. He had to track thousands of members, multiple contracts, and various committees, plus handle hundreds of calls a day and be able to change course on a dime.

"See you in about an hour, Dick." They had reached the corner of Adams and Clark. Parker waved good-bye as he walked onto Plymouth Court.

★   ★   ★

"Parker, it's always a pleasure." Ben was standing straight and tall in his tailored gray suit. He was all of five foot four inches. He looked up at Parker.

"Ben. Thanks for this." They walked up the stairs and into the dining room of the Standard Club.

The tables were well separated for private discussions in the large, elegant dining room. Within seconds, freshly squeezed orange juice was poured and a waiter was bringing Ben his usual bowl of fruit and Parker his usual bowl of oatmeal. The entitlements came daily in this life. No real hardships.

"Parker, I know this is a busy time for you, but I want to make sure we're on track for a quick round of negotiations with the hospital. You know I'm a firm supporter of the unions, and I believe we can make it a win-win for both sides." Ben sat straight in his chair. Never slouching, he was meticulously neat and never missed a word in between chews of his strawberries and blackberries in their yogurt gravy.

"We're with you, Ben. My labor staff there has a very good track record, and we already know our issues are easily solvable. Sounds like the governor wishes to make both sides happy." Parker was mixing brown sugar into his oats.

"Yes. Congratulations on being to the governor's right. That's a big-time place, Parker. People notice."

"They do."

"Lots of people see you going far, Parker. Can you play this game?"

"Yes. But do I want to?"

"That's an interesting answer, Mr. Moore." Ben put down his spoon and precisely wiped his mouth with his cloth napkin held in both hands. "Once you're in, it's not like you can just leave. That doesn't go over well in these circles—and they make sure you don't come back." Ben was looking around the room. A smile on his face. He turned to Parker and looked him in the eye. "And you're now in."

"Thank you, Ben. We'll have the contract done in three sessions."

"That's what I like to hear. Good press makes me a rich man."

Ben gets rich while I get more enemies that want me gone. Parker smiled a fake smile and thought about how he should go over to the dark side and make it all about the money.

"Just glad I got to the governor's right side, Ben." Parker finished his juice and the two began to stand.

"Oh, Parker. Be careful with the county commissioners. Everyone's heard what you said in public about the board president's approach to health care in his county. Everyone is connected in this state. You may be in, but this is Chicago." Ben shook Parker's hand as they exited the dining room.

★ ★ ★

"Carlos. Good morning." Parker had walked a block over to his building and swiped his ID at the desk.

"Morning, Mr. Moore. You looked good on TV yesterday."

"Thanks, Carlos."

Parker didn't have to wait for an elevator. Carlos punched the board and one opened immediately as he walked over. Parker knew what Carlos did.

"Thanks." Parker waved at the smiling security guard. Parker was in.

Chapter 18

When Parker walked into the office, everyone was busy. Brenda was on the phone at the front desk and only waved. Parker walked down the hall and into his office. He sat at his desk and started going through the pile of mail Brenda had left. Pete walked in and sat behind him at the table with several notebooks in hand.

"You ready, Parker? I'll be right back with some coffee."

Parker turned his computer on and quickly went to his e-mail. There were always rants from one union steward at one of the public hospitals that would be written at three in the morning. He wondered if she ever slept. As he waited for Pete, he noticed another e-mail listed as previously read. It was from a contact at SEIU, same as before.

"Here we go." Pete placed two mugs of coffee on the table.

"Thanks, Pete." Parker got up and walked over. The pleasantries of the morning and the easy life took his mind off a wife somewhere in Florida. *But the e-mail?*

"So, here's our financials from the hospital and here's what the members are going to the table with."

"I never thought I'd see the day we were winning contracts for nurses, and they'd be bitching about making ninety to a hundred thousand dollars a year." Parker rubbed his forehead as he scrutinized the spreadsheets.

"They say it's not the money, but the overtime."

"Bullshit. Let's take the money off the table and see what they say."

The two men spent the next hour hatching strategy for the members to begin taking more responsibility for their negotiations. It seemed to empower them and led to a better margin of victory on the final vote.

★ ★ ★

"Tell the governor it's a sure thing. I wouldn't trust Moore. He's not there yet."

"Well, thank you for that and the donation. We'll make sure the legislation works for your facility." The governor's lobbyist hung up the phone after talking to Ben Flarrety. He dialed a number with an area code in Ingham County, Michigan.

"Hello?" A woman answered.

"Are you still down there?"

★ ★ ★

Parker worked the rest of the week without incident. Dick dropped him off late Thursday afternoon in his driveway. The four-hour drive back to Ingham County was the usual conversation about the Detroit Tigers, White Castle hamburgers, and how many games the Lions would lose come fall. Interspersed between topics, were the multiple calls Parker would get from constituents and members all over Illinois with problems or complaints. There was never a pleasant conversation.

Parker didn't look in the garage to see if her truck was inside. The house was a mess. "Anybody home?"

Silence.

He noticed the luggage upstairs sitting open on the bed. Parker sat down on the bed and looked out the window to the side gardens he had planted. He was home until Monday. He lay down on the bed and closed his eyes wishing he'd awake to laughter and happiness.

Hours later he was in the boy's room with the door locked while she screamed at him from their bedroom. The next morning he got up and came downstairs. He made coffee and walked out to the rose garden and sat on the bench he had bought for her.

After ten minutes, she came outside with a cup of coffee. She wore a G-string and one of his shirts.

"No kids this weekend. How about we spend the morning in bed?" She leaned against his shoulder as they both gazed over the back field through the bird sanctuary Parker had built.

This is how it was. Never an apology. Never a discussion of the previous night. It was yelling or sex. In between, Parker worked in the garden or tied flies for the fishing trips he couldn't go on anymore. There was always the good, like some golf and dancing on a Friday or Saturday night down at the Exchange nightclub in Lansing. But it was always an attempt to prevent the next fury. There wasn't a loving mode. It was a dance around the dysfunction.

Chapter 19

On the train Monday, Parker worked on some reports and watched a movie on his laptop. The calls usually started about 7:00 a.m. Legislative calls would come first, while everyone got their days planned out early. There was a frantic tone when the Illinois legislature was in session. Michigan had a full-time legislature so ideas and bills lagged. In Illinois, bills flew at breakneck speed, and by the end of the day, some issues were pulled completely off the table and the next issues were being set up for the next day.

And, there was always the money. A constant stream of fundraising calls and favors done for groups the legislators favored. Anything to get in their good graces.

Parker continued to work through his dissonance within the crooked and legendary political system of Chicago and Illinois and was amazed at the amount of influence each group built upon the other: the connections from boards of directors, to CEOs through their attorneys, and finally to the legislators. The average American had absolutely no idea how government really worked—it was *not* by electing specific people to specific positions.

Multi-client lobby firms had the skids greased and the mythical machine existed. Parker learned how groups from foreign countries were beginning to work their way into these firms. Even the major media networks played the game because that is where the money was. Everyone took part, while the common man was losing everything. Just enough money trickled down to the wanna-bes for their McMansions and SUVs so that most stayed happy.

Sandy Garner of Garner and Associates phoned as soon as Parker walked in after his usual stop at the Rookery. Garner and Associates, the company's contracted multi-client lobby firm, had worked all weekend since the Illinois legislature was in session.

"Parker, we have some issues with your legislative platform. The governor's staff has made it very clear: you get what you want if you make it worth the governor's time."

"How much?" He knew the game. He remembered the words of the mystery man and the governor at the last press conference. They also knew he had a PAC meeting in two days. The words he would hear over and over from the governor, "Parker, we need ya. The support of your folks is important to us, so keep letting me know where everyone is on the chart. Can't have anyone jumping ship." The governor would pull Parker aside at every press conference and speaking engagement. They were never in-depth conversations, instead they were shallow and about who was backing who. Subjects of legislation were left to the governor's leaders in the State House and Senate or his staff, which was mostly made up of campaign leaders. The governor enjoyed making appearances.

"They're asking for ten thousand," Sandy said.

"You're kidding me. He won't settle the state contract for our group but he will sign legislation for the private sector *if*, and I mean *if*, we get him money. I'm supposed to sell this to people on his payroll who are working thirty hours straight and taking pay cuts?"

Sandy stammered. She had lots of legislation on the line for many clients. She had to come through for the governor or none of her clients would be happy. The greatest difficulty with multi-client firms was that they picked and chose their battles but made it look like your decision. Lobbyists were an interesting group. Extremely intelligent to follow several subjects and track them through governmental systems, but they quietly worked with their groups one separate from the other. If a lobby firm had a big piece of legislation, or a regulation pending or under discussion for a large firm paying lots of money, it was guaranteed the lower-paying clients would have to make concessions for their interests to keep everyone happy. The legislators knew the game too. Deals were made all the time based on where the money was coming from.

"Look, we've got solid backing on all of our bills, but the party will follow the governor's lead," she said.

"This is bullshit," Parker barked. "I'm going to call him personally."

Silence.

Parker did not like the multi-client groups. They were gutless when challenges came down the pike in a legislative battle. Sandy had left him hanging out to dry in one recent Senate hearing. It was against the governor's labor staff and she knew it was a no-win situation. Suddenly, one of her other clients needed her, so she begged off. Parker showed up with three people to testify, but was challenged by another labor union and the governor's sharks prior to the meeting. Before they went into chambers, the challenge became heated. Parker told them all to fuck off. The governor's senior staff member went to the Senate Chair and told him what had occurred. The hearing was cancelled. Sandy knew the plan and didn't want to risk a bad day with the governor's group. Parker had to take the brunt of the anger.

"Look," Sandy continued, "you know very well the governor won't take that call or discuss what I'm telling you. This is coming from someone high up in his office. Everyone's getting hammered."

"Well, I don't take well to being hammered or bribed. Thanks, Sandy. I'll get back with you." Parker wanted to slam down the receiver but stopped and pretended to throw the phone out the window. There she was. Today it was blue jeans, a tan t-shirt, and high heels.

"What the fuck do you want?" Parker yelled out his open window as he stood up and leaned on his desk.

Brenda was passing by his office door and peeked.

"Parker, are you okay?"

"Fine."

He abruptly sat down without turning to acknowledge her.

"Okay then," Brenda said quietly and continued down the hallway.

"Why do they dress her like Stefanie? I sure as hell hope you Super PAC bozos are getting this." Parker kept talking to himself.

He put the receiver in the cradle and looked outside toward the federal courthouse to his right. He was beginning to understand why they had built a high-rise federal prison in downtown Chicago.

Chapter 20

Parker rented a car and drove down to Springfield the Tuesday night before the PAC meeting. He didn't notice anyone following him, but that didn't surprise him. If it was the governor's people, they knew where he was going.

He checked into the Crowne Plaza Hotel on South Dirksen Parkway. The hotel always gave Parker the state rate since he had so many union members that worked in the state health-care system, and the beds were big enough so his feet wouldn't hang over the edge. One of the little luxuries in his life.

On the way up the stairs to the registration desk, he noticed Todd Ramsey dressed in a suit having a beer in the bar.

"Mr. Jones. National Exports right?"

"Why, yes. How can I help you?"

"May I sit?"

"Please."

"How long do we keep this up?" Parker whispered as he motioned for the bartender.

"Let's just have a beer and talk sports. My room is next to the one you're going to get," Ramsey whispered back as he shoved some peanuts into his mouth and never took his eyes off the TV.

"Going to get? You guys are amazing." Parker smiled and looked up at the Cardinals-Cubs game.

"What'll it be?" The bartender had arrived.

"Are you buying, Mr. Jones?"

"Sure, why not."

"I'll have the Lagavulin. Snifter. No ice."

"Pretentious bastard," Ramsey said, still looking up at the game.

The two finished their drinks as they watched the ballgame that went into extra innings. Albert Pujols ended it in the eleventh inning with a two-run dinger.

"Well, thank you, Mr. Jones. It's been a pleasure." Parker got up, shook Ramsey's hand, and went to the registration desk.

Todd Ramsey exited the bar and went to the elevators well ahead of Parker. He made his way to the 8th floor and into his room. Once inside, he opened the adjoining suite door and sat down in a chair to wait for Parker's arrival.

Parker made his way to the 8th floor and opened his room door.

"Mr. Jones, I didn't realize we were married."

"You better be glad we are, Moore. There's a lot of shit going on down here, and we may have to get you out soon." Ramsey sat back in the chair with his legs crossed.

"No shit. Do you finally believe I'm being followed?" Parker sat on the bed.

"More than that. We've been watching and listening to the FBI down here. We're not sure if it's them playing with you, the county wanting to get rid of you, or the governor's staff setting you up for something they don't want you to talk about."

"The county's easy. I'll be dodging them for a while." Parker took off his shoes and began to change into his sweats. "The FBI?"

"They've been working with the State Attorney General. She's got a hard-on for the governor. Nothing public yet other than the cascade of hate talk between them."

"Are you trying to tell me they might be setting me up for blackmail?" Parker had finished changing and was putting pillows together behind his back on the bed.

"Blackmail or something. You've already donated to some of his favorites, right?"

"Yes. You guys knew about that when you visited me in Michigan."

"Well, there's gonna be more. We'll just have to see what it is."

"More than the ten thousand he's asking for?"

"Absolutely. You cave and that's just the beginning."

"You want us to cave?"

"Absolutely."

★　★　★

She made her way into the Crowne Plaza after being dropped off. She went to the registration desk and shook the desk attendant's hand while she held a one hundred dollar bill.

"Mr. Moore's room, please." She smiled and leaned over the counter, showing as much cleavage as she could. Her blonde hair fell long over the backless black dress that came well above her thigh. Her stiletto heels placed her at least three inches taller than the attendant.

"Sure. Eight twenty-three."

"Thanks, sweetie." She leaned into the attendant and pecked him on the cheek.

★　★　★

Ramsey stood up and walked toward his room.

"Just be careful, Parker. If the FBI gets too close to what we're doing, we'll have to get you outta here."

"Thanks, Todd. Don't be too far away."

Ramsey shut the door behind him and headed for the shower.

The knock on Parker's door came several minutes after Ramsey left. He was still in his sweats and flipping through the TV channels. He kept trying to reach Stefanie by phone, but it went to voicemail each time. The clock at his bedside said 11:43 p.m.

"You didn't have to …" It wasn't Ramsey at the door. "What the hell are you doing here?"

Chapter 21

She didn't say anything and walked into Parker's room.

"May I?" she asked as she sat down on the bed.

Parker shut the door and walked past the bed to the chair. He sat back with his hands in his lap, legs stretched out, and feet crossed. Ramsey's words were fresh in his mind.

"For what do I owe this honor?" he asked looking at the striking figure. She was leaning back on both hands. Her head was turned toward him and softly angled like a magazine model doing a photo shoot.

"The governor thought we should introduce ourselves. He thinks maybe you might be getting the wrong idea."

"You've been watching me for two weeks. What other idea should I get?"

"That we're actually trying to protect you."

"From?"

"People.

"People?"

"Some people might be trying to make your life uncomfortable. We can make that go away." She got up and stood over Parker.

"How could you do that?"

"Well, I could …" She spread her legs and lowered herself slowly, straddling Parker, and began whispering in his ear.

"That's certainly protection." Parker wasn't smiling, but he wasn't frowning. He had taken off his wire when changing. She was kissing his cheek.

She stood up, turned, and began to pull her dress over her head. When it got up over her eyes, Parker stood and pulled it back down.

"What the hell? Not good enough for you? Your wife would approve."

"Now I know you're nuts. Thank you, but no."

"Coward."

"That's one thing I'm not." He pushed her gently to the door. "Please tell the governor, or whoever you work for, that I'm good for the money."

"Fine. No skin off my back."

"No dress either."

"It would have been fun."

"Amazing actually, but some other time."

She walked out the door. Parker closed and locked it.

"Blackmail," he said to himself.

Chapter 22

Wednesday the union's PAC met in their Springfield office. Parker and Sandy were there, along with the PAC Chair who also happened to be the union's treasurer.

"What's this about the governor and ten thousand dollars?" The treasurer was always briefed by Parker prior to the meetings so she could act knowledgeable.

"He's telling everyone that to get whatever you want through the legislature and signed by him, you have to contribute to his campaign," said Sandy.

"Isn't that illegal?" asked one of the elder retired union members.

"It doesn't matter," Sandy responded. "We have several bills in our legislative package; you just need to ask yourself if you want them or not."

Parker always became conscious of the wire when the conversation became controversial.

"The governor is flat-out bribing us." Parker wasn't being diplomatic. He thought about what he said and added, "Look, I don't like this, but I suspect this is how business is done now." He looked over at Sandy, who was nodding. She was desperate for a yes answer from this group for the benefit of the rest of her clients.

"I think we'd give him the money anyway; so maybe it's just the motive." The treasurer was being honest, but from someone who wanted to be union president, she would say anything to gain support from both sides.

"I agree," a member chimed in.

"Let's vote now and at least get a picture of where we're at. Those in favor of the ten thousand dollar donation raise your hand." The treasurer was all business.

All the PAC members raised their hands.

"Okay. I guess it's done. Parker, you'll just have to go around the state and sell it because we're doing it," said the treasurer.

The rest of the meeting was taken up by Sandy telling the PAC members which candidates were leading in their respective House and Senate races and whom the group should send money to. It was never about principle. It was about backing the winner so a voice could be bought. There was always hell to pay if the candidate who won wasn't backed by the PAC. Legislators knew what lists groups were on, thus money was divided as evenly as possible to candidates of both parties and even to both candidates in the same race. Parker's union clients didn't have the money the banks, pharmaceuticals, and foreign countries could afford to give candidates, but those groups did the same thing. It was always divided in the name of influence. What made the union money a little more disturbing was the federal law covering PACs. Dues were not supposed to pay for political campaigns. The accountants were always challenged with the bookkeeping.

Parker was angry. It was a decision he wished they wouldn't have made, especially without the full union's approval, but the NSA would be happy. He would be the one to get flak from every member in the State of Illinois. Add this to the usual abuse he received at home, and Parker was really caught in a grist mill.

"I'll get the checks cut and we'll start making the deliveries." Parker was sitting at the table talking to Sandy as the members made their way out of the office.

"Look Parker, I know this is hard for you …" Sandy began.

"This part is hard because it makes no common sense. I've been in this business for a long time now, and it has gotten less about principle and more about the money. That's what I don't like."

"I don't know what to say."

"We all make money connected to it, Sandy. You guys make a boat load and so do I. Now if you'll excuse me, I've got a meeting the governor asked me to attend at the Capitol."

"Yes, I know. I'm going with you."

"Fine."

They walked out of the office and down the side alley which used to be a street between taverns back in the 1800s. The bricks were still intact in the road.

"Do you know what this is about?" Parker was glad he wore a short-sleeved shirt under his suit. The Springfield humidity was catching up to him.

"It's about us cooperating with his labor folks. We'll get everything we're asking for on the private side, but he's probably going to fight you on the contracts for state employees."

"What? Did you talk to him after our phone conversation?"

"No. Not him, but I'm trying to help you with his staff."

"That kinda help I don't need, Sandy. Let me carry the messages about the union."

"That's what you're doing today. I guess I'll take a rain check. Do you mind?"

Parker thought about it before he said anything. She'd left him hanging before. It's about her looking good, not Parker or his group.

"No. Not at all. I'll catch up with you afterward at Augie's—and you're buying."

"Fair enough. See you later. Call me." Sandy went around to the backside of the Capitol.

Once through security, Parker took a side elevator to the second floor. He went to the East Wing and through the glass doors leading into the governor's office.

"Mr. Moore. Yes, they've been waiting for you. This way." The secretary led Parker to the formal office. "Here you go, sir. Can I get you some coffee?"

"Thank you. That would be great."

Sitting at the table were most of the governor's brain trust. His main advisor, who also doubled as campaign manager, his labor directors, and some other people Parker didn't know. There was no governor. Parker wasn't late, but they'd obviously been talking before he arrived.

"Mr. Moore, there's a seat for you over there." The advisor pointed to a chair across from the labor director. It was the only chair on that side of the table. The advisor leaned on the table between two other people. "We'd like to talk to you about the upcoming contracts."

"Okay." Parker looked over at the advisor. "Oh, thank you," he said as his coffee was placed in front of him.

"We're going to be honest with you. There's not a lot of wiggle room here." The advisor was now pacing behind his contingent of people. "We know we've all done great work to assist the private side of health care in Illinois, after all, that's big business. One hundred and twenty-one facilities around Chicago alone and that's a lot of employers and employees."

More about the votes, Parker thought. He listened to the man drone on for a few minutes about the prisons, state psychiatric hospitals, the forensic center, and other parts of the state's system.

"That's all well and good, Mr. Peabody, but if this is an attempt to have me negotiate privately, away from my members at those locations, we can end this meeting right now."

"Did I imply that? We were just looking to … "

"To what? Get me to agree to things so the governor can get off the hook and let me get taken to the woodshed? Sorry."

"I would suggest, Mr. Moore, that you follow the dictates before you and cooperate with us."

"Back in Michigan, I'd get hanged for this."

"Michigan? Let me tell you something. You are in Illinois not Michigan." He walked close to Parker and bent down into Parker's face. "Fuck Michigan."

"I think we're done here." Parker stood up and looked at the governor's advisor. "Thanks for the coffee." He left the room and walked out of the double-glass doors of the governor's office without looking back.

Chapter 23

"Lagavulin."

"I know. Snifter, no ice." Harry, the bartender at Augie's, was already reaching for the scotch.

"Sandy, what are you drinking?"

"What should I get, Parker?"

"Hemlock."

"Nice. It went that well, eh?"

"Better. They know they're getting their money."

"Did you tell them?"

"I told a friend of theirs last night."

"Who?"

"Just a mutual friend. They got the message."

"Okay. So you're going to be in cars, trains, and planes the next little while."

"Me and John Candy. Hope he doesn't lose track of his pillows." Parker took a sniff of the single malt set in front of him.

"Moore, what the hell are you talking about?" Sandy pointed at the Grey Goose vodka. "On the rocks, Harry."

"Nothing. How about them Bears?"

"How much of that have you already had?"

"Got here just before you did, Sandy. This is my first. I have one more stop after this."

Count Basie was playing *Chicago* in the background.

"Parker, you are a mystery sometimes, but I will say you do get the job done."

"So, Sandy. When are you going to stop setting me up for your benefit?" He drank some scotch. "Did you tell them we had a PAC meeting today?"

Sandy set her drink down and looked at Parker with an indignant smirk. "Set you up? Set you up? I'm the one who's gotta clean up your messes." She looked at the mirror behind the bar and took a long drink of her vodka. "Anybody could have told him about the meeting. You have thousands of members out there, Moore. Besides, the governor wasn't going to be there today."

Ella Fitzgerald and Cole Porter took over in the background.

"Yeah. I guess that's true. Please stop setting up the messes." Parker finished his scotch and plopped down some money on the bar; then took it back. "Oh, that's right. You clean up my messes. Clean up this one." He pushed the bar stool away so hard it almost fell.

★   ★   ★

Peabody finished his call to the governor after Parker's exit. He dialed another number.

"Are you back?"

"I've been back and doing my part. You are getting your money's worth, believe me. I'm in his e-mails and in his head."

"You really are crazy, aren't you?"

"No. I just like what I like and will do anything to get it. Period."

★   ★   ★

Parker drove to the Crowne Plaza and made his way up to his room. He began by taking his tie off and knocking at the adjoining room door.

"Back."

The door opened. Ramsey came in sans suit. Today it was jeans and a t-shirt.

"Everything go okay today?" Ramsey asked.

"I don't know. You tell me. You hear everything."

"It's not always me, Parker. How'd it go?"

"I suspect perfect. They're getting their money. I'll look bad. The other lobbyists get to keep their clients happy, and I get to go home to the unknown borderline."

"Borderline?"

"Yes. That's what I'm living with and that's what I'm becoming. My whole fucking life is borderline. No truth. No life. No empathy. Just drama that everyone keeps feeding off of."

"Where you going?"

"Home. I'm supposed to keep score at George's hockey game tonight in Ann Arbor."

"Ann Arbor? Are you nuts? That's like seven hours away, and you're due back in Chicago tomorrow."

"Six if you drive really fast. I can make it right before game time at eight." Parker was changed and throwing stuff into his small travel bag. "My kids are my only sanity. Tonight, I need sanity."

"Take it easy. We're not done with you yet."

Parker was almost to the door and turned around. He looked at Ramsey leaning against the doorway to the adjoining suite.

"By the way, you're welcome. Do you know by the end of this day everybody except me will have exactly what they want—and do you think I heard a thank you from anyone? I'll see you tomorrow." He threw the wire at Ramsey and shut the door behind him; realizing it was the third time that day he'd walked out on someone.

Chapter 24

Parker jumped in his car and headed to east I-55. He tried calling Stefanie's cell, but realized she was at work and hung up. He dialed her office and got the message machine.

He put in a CD and Bob Seger's "Turn the Page" came through the speakers. Parker played that song after every long day of meetings, speaking events, and presentations. He drove 80 mph not worrying about any cop. He'd just stop and then go 80 mph again.

As he listened to the music, he thought of the Gnostic Gospel of Thomas. Theory has it that it was written by the Apostle 'Doubting' Thomas.

> Blessed is the lion whom the man devours, for that lion will become man. But cursed is the man whom the lion devours, for that man shall become lion.

Parker was devolving into a lion. He could feel himself losing everything he held dear to his heart and soul. He struggled with a higher plane. A power not to catapult himself, but to enlighten. To have others around him enjoy life more and realize one works to live not lives to work. Yet he was constantly at work. His home life and respite was an emotionally charged unpredictability—just like his job. He was becoming as borderline as the personalities around him. He fought to keep the last vestiges of a healthy person— empathy.

He was losing track of how his actions, emotions, and decisions affected those around him; people who trusted him to do the right thing for their welfare. Decisions that could affect a job, a family, how money was spent at the corner grocery store, everything at these levels affected millions indirectly. He spent his days amongst people who didn't care. It was about the inner circle and their own egos and appearances. The higher the influence you peddled the more lives you affected; however, the colder in nature you had to become.

That was the paradox. He did empathize, and it was killing him. His life had become one of multiple personalities. No longer was the man devouring the lion, but the lion devouring man. Parker was around a million people—and felt more lonely than ever.

★　★　★

For the next six months, Parker traveled from Cairo to Elgin and from Quincy to Kankakee. He got the buy-in for the governor's payout and felt slimy the whole time. His board believed it was the right thing to do, only because they didn't want to lose their power and influence. Parker was now convinced unions were no better than any other groups. They needed their victories and their members' dues—the hell with what was right. When Parker met with the union members and got them to approve the signing of the check for the governor's campaign fund, they didn't know he was wearing a wire, and they didn't know there was already talk about who would buy the Senate seat that would be vacated if a popular senator from Illinois was elected President of the United States.

Each time Parker sat in on a PAC meeting, the NSA agents picked up the information. The next part of the game involved special events and private parties. Parker or Sandy would arrange for the meet-and-greet, and the checks ended up in the hands of the appropriate legislators. In Illinois, it was always easy. The reality of one group influencing one party more than the other was a media ruse. Everybody shared the money, and no one cared where or from whom the money came as long as it went into the PAC. Once there, it looked like it came from one group.

He never saw the blonde shadow and never met with Mr. Peabody again. The money was flowing well enough.

Chapter 25

One night during his six month of travels, he met with Cindy, the union steward from the University of Chicago Hospital. They were seated in a booth at the Italian Village on Monroe Street in Chicago; Sandy and Cindy faced Parker. The booth was in the rear of the upper level and was covered on three sides by walls. Parker had just motioned for the waiter to refresh their drinks. His Lagavulin was perfect for the night's conversation. The steward was concerned that her nursing colleagues continued to work mandatory overtime on the patient units, resulting in sixteen-, eighteen-, and twenty-hour shifts.

"It's not that they don't like the money, but they have kids and families to tend to. We didn't sign up for this. Twelve hours is enough. When somebody makes a mistake due to fatigue, either a patient suffers or the employee, or both. It's not like we're making widgets. We can't afford to make mistakes. The residents and interns get to take naps and snooze as much as they can. We can't. We have a nurse who works every day. She is making more money than any other city employee—and this is Chicago!"

Cindy was getting louder with each sentence as she voiced the hospitals' dirty secret: fewer staff was a gamble worth taking because most nurses would not make mistakes that would result in huge lawsuits. So, hospitals kept staff costs down and margins up, knowing if they had to pay off a patient it was still less money than fully staffing the units on a daily basis.

"When can we expect the relief from the governor that he keeps promising?" Cindy was leaning forward and feeling the Long Island Iced Teas.

"We can guarantee some relief soon," Sandy said quietly. She was nearing the end of her first decade as a lobbyist. She was more protective of her career as a whole, meaning she couldn't take a real stand for any one client lest she piss off either the governor or legislature and place her other clients at risk. In Illinois, it was all about perception, not reality.

"Actually, Cindy," Parker chimed in, after giving Sandy an angry look, "we just cut a deal with our good governor." Parker was aware of the wire again. Oftentimes it was so much a part of him he gave it no thought. Tonight, he felt like grabbing it and talking into it like a microphone on a stage. "We'll get our legislation through and signed, no problem." Parker looked around. The Italian Village was the perfect restaurant for this discussion. "All of you will be able to attend the signing downtown. He won't do it in Springfield."

"Maybe we shouldn't be so confident, Parker." Sandy was staring daggers at him. Her voice was as tight as the sphincters she was trying to hold together.

"We've guaranteed money for the governor's re-election campaign, so he agreed to stop holding up our bills." Parker never told Cindy the amount, knowing that information would come later.

"Great! Whatever it takes. This is Illinois!" She chuckled.

Sandy wasn't happy with Parker for being so open about the deal, but Parker didn't care. She was not driving around the state getting the union members to agree. She was not the one who sat in the parking lots of hospitals, prisons, clinics, and late-night coffee shops to be screamed at by irate people of all political persuasions.

The real irony of the night was their dining at the Italian Village. The restaurant opened in 1927 at the height of the Chicago gang scene. The booth had red-velvet walls and cushions, dark lighting, and barriers for limited vision if you were trying to sneak a peek on who was inside. The bar, as you walked upstairs and turned to the left, looked like something Al Capone would sit at to flash his power to anyone who ventured in, and then the darkness of the booths in the rear would hear the quiet discussions of the night. Parker thought it interesting that some eighty years later the discussions had changed from gangster to governor but still involved handing over money.

Chapter 26

Parker hand delivered the $10,000 check, and the next day television cameras showed the governor signing health-care legislation, including laws that cleared the way for college scholarships, provided for more professionals in hospitals, and would make health care better. All a ruse. The governor had no money to pay for any of it, but he got his check.

The same occurred in Michigan years before. The senator from Michigan was no different than the governor of Illinois except for the hair and gender. The political and economic machines just kept running.

★   ★   ★

Parker drove home on Thursday evening. With the amount of driving required lately, he was using the train less. He always made sure he was home four or five nights a week. After the long, six-hour trip, he ended up in a violent argument with Stefanie after being berated for not calling enough.

No, "Hello, sweetie, you must be tired." No, "It's so good to have you home."

Parker went into a kid's room and locked the door. He climbed into the twin bed and fell asleep. She continued to yell from the other room.

Chapter 27

Word reached the governor and his staff that Parker was unhappy about the money exchange for legislation. For all Parker knew, it was his lobby firm that spread the tale. Sandy knew how to make sure people experienced the wrath of the political machine when she felt wronged.

One day, Parker stood in the middle of the Capitol rotunda in Springfield, Illinois. He romanticized what times must have been like before Abe Lincoln's presidential election. Parker had to meet with the State Senate Majority Leader who was the governor's henchwoman. He approached the senator with a smile as she walked through the rotunda, but she put her right index finger under his nose and began to yell about the budget and how Parker should remember who signed legislation. She had just been at a labor meeting which included the state's labor representative and the governor's advisor/campaign manager. They were unhappy that Parker challenged them on not providing for state employees while passing and signing similar legislation for private-sector workers—and that Parker had actually used the word *bribery* connected to the ten thousand dollars.

"Do you hear me?" she screamed.

"Yes, Ma'am, but …" Parker wasn't sure what he heard. His mind reverted back to the nightly tirades at home. "I'm only doing my job and what's best for the people of Illinois. You remember, the people who voted for you and the governor?" Parker knew he was making her angrier but she couldn't reply to his statement. He also noticed the hundreds of school children and other visitors observing the exchange in silence.

"You just watch yourself." She looked around and noted the audience. She turned to Parker and whispered, "Or it's all going to end." She hustled her way toward the Senate chambers, smiling to everyone and stopping to shake hands with some children.

Parker watched her and found himself getting more and more angry. He went to the cafeteria in the basement of the Capitol where he found Sandy eating a sandwich. As soon as he made eye contact with her, he could tell she didn't want him anywhere near her.

"Just got done chatting with your best friend, the senator. I can't believe how you're never around when the bullets are flying." Parker plopped himself down across from her.

Sandy said nothing and kept chewing. After she swallowed, she took a drink of Coke and looked around the room. She leaned in toward Parker.

"I know there's a lot of shit right now, but all of our clients are going through it. You're the only one trying to fight it. Why? Both sides are getting what they want."

"Do you think this is right? Don't you think at some point this is going to blow up?"

"If it does, we all run for cover. You know that. Once you leave this business or someone is ousted for not following the norm, you're gone. Poof. Like you never existed. But those of us who stay, just go quiet. We do our jobs …"

"And keep collecting the money. Yeah, I get it."

"Look, Moore, what do you want from me? I'm a lobbyist. It's what we do. It's not like you're wanting for much. Trophy wife, kids, home, vacations, you name it, you got it."

At face value, Sandy was right. Most everyone thought Parker had it made. It was his own disconnect that drove him nuts. If only he had a quiet home life, maybe he could do this with a different perspective.

"Sandy, I should tell you something." Parker actually thought about spilling his guts. "What you see isn't always what is real."

She could sense Parker was serious. His head was bent toward the table. No eye contact. He slouched down in his chair. For once, she actually showed the possibility of understanding. Parker caught himself.

"No. Never mind."

"Parker, what is it?"

"No. Thanks for listening; and I'm sorry I've been a little short lately. I'll see you later." Parker got up and smiled at Sandy.

"Take it easy, Parker. None of this is personal, you know?"

"I have trouble separating it, Sandy. It's all personal. Don't let anybody fool you."

Parker walked away and realized he was the only one saying thank you.

★   ★   ★

A month later, the State Senate Majority Leader looked forward to Parker's visit to her office. She greeted him with a hug and a smile. He had a five thousand dollar check from the union's PAC for her campaign fund and that didn't include the money from individual members he'd called in for their personal donations. Little did Parker know, his challenges of the Illinois governor would be much more serious once the FBI investigated similar situations in the state. He began to wonder how protected he was from real threats. Did people know who he worked for? As the rumors swelled about what was going on in Illinois, Parker never stopped looking over his shoulder. It was becoming a way of life.

★   ★   ★

The heart palpitations started as soon as he handed off the wire to Ramsey on a backstreet in the south side of Chicago, and then headed for home. Through Gary, Indiana, and on toward Michigan City, they worsened. Sometimes he'd sweat, and sometimes he'd try listening to music. That night, Parker faced horrid yelling and screaming. He again spent the night in one of the kid's rooms with the door locked.

Depression and anger were stirring deep inside and taking their toll on Parker's ability to function, let alone exist.

Chapter 28

As the legislative season continued into 2007, after the governor successfully held onto his office in 2006, Parker was working with his labor executive, Pete. They were in the middle of contentious negotiations with the University of Chicago Hospital. To make matters worse, one of the attorneys Parker was supposed to build a relationship with, according to the NSA, was on the hospital's payroll. He was the perfect labor attorney–for the anti-union forces. He'd call Parker and want to have quiet lunches to seduce Parker with stories of how bad a job Pete was doing and how unhappy all the union members were. Parker just kept checking the stories with Pete and the other staff. Parker wanted to keep the attorney close and not simply tell him to take a hike. Parker played the game right up until the union members voted down the contract.

Parker was mortified. How could Pete, with his years of experience, misjudge the vote? It was a three-to-one vote against. Pete's nickname was Ice Pick. He'd been with the Teamsters for ten years, but got into a political dispute and was let go. Parker hired him at the first interview based on his experience, knowledge of Chicago, and personality. Parker felt Pete needed a fresh start, but after one year, Pete lost that first contract vote at the University of Chicago. The union members were angry with Pete, so Parker worked twenty hours a day for four months to turn the vote. As the executive director, Parker needed to fix it and get Pete back on track. The union business worked like no other. Once out of favor, you may never find an inroad again. It was unforgiving, and the gossip channels were like a London tabloid.

It was an early summer afternoon. Parker answered the phone. The union's vice president was tired of the gossip.

"Fire him," she said.

"Why?" Parker asked. He knew who the vice president meant.

"Fire him. You make me happy, then you're happy. I'm not happy, you don't have a job." The voice was stern.

Parker didn't know what to say. He'd heard stories of CEOs and executives receiving orders from boards, but he'd never had to face it. Even after sixteen years in the executive suite. With this threat, Parker had no solace at work or at home. He had run out of safe places.

"Well …" he hesitated.

"No. You don't have a choice."

Parker didn't hear the dial tone. He held the phone to his ear as he looked due east at the Chicago Museum of Art on Michigan Avenue. It used to be one of his favorite views. Now, even that pleasure was crumbling. Which was the greatest threat? The union vice president or a former Teamster named Ice Pick? It didn't matter. Both would threaten his life for years.

★   ★   ★

Parker took his wife to Chicago for the weekend in yet another vain attempt to change her. Stefanie loved the excitement of the city and never found fault with their nights out at the blues clubs on Clark, the games at Wrigley Field, or the expensive dinners— many of which were paid for by local attorneys for favors. In fact, the weekends in Chicago were often better than those spent home. Unfortunately, Parker just kept sinking further and further into the boiling water.

They were sitting at the bar of the Capital Grille on St. Clair Street after entertaining some union members. Parker was talking with Tim, the bartender. Stefanie got up and went to the restroom while Parker turned and surveyed the dinner crowd. When he turned back toward the bar, there were four shots of tequila, two other women, and a smiling Tim. At that moment, Stefanie came around the corner and Parker's throat tightened. Tim was just about to hand Stefanie one of the tequila shots and toast his two friends at the bar, when he saw her glare at Parker. The two women drank their shots and left as fast as they could.

Tim simply looked at Parker and mouthed the words "I'm sorry."

Ten minutes later, she was berating Parker through the crowded sidewalks of downtown Chicago. For some unknown reason, she began to call Parker's oldest daughter a bitch. He just kept walking toward the car. Her anger intensified as he drove to the apartment in Evanston. As soon as he parked, he threw her the key, got out of the car, and went through the locked gate to the apartment. She only had the car key. She couldn't get past the iron gates. Parker went up to the apartment and didn't take her calls for the next two days. She drove home to Michigan. That weekend, he watched the 1959 movie *The Bad Seed*. He thought it was perfect for his life at this time. The only problem was finding the right dock to end the story.

Chapter 29

Parker rode the train home on Monday morning and skipped work. He would return to Chicago on Tuesday and work through Friday.

He worked on the landscaping of their home for hours. The yard would come to be known by his friends as Parker Park. It included a football area, lacrosse and badminton nets, swings, a tree house, sandbox, and a third of an acre for a bird sanctuary filled with boxes and feeders of all shapes and sizes. The backyard gardens overflowed with stella d'oro and day lilies, shrubs, mums, zinnias, assorted perennials, and two rose gardens complete with a boulder and a bench. Working outside on the landscape was tiring but rewarding. It had become a hobby of solitude for Parker.

He was walking across the driveway by the front of the garage. Before he could react, the Envoy backed into him. He fell to the ground. Stunned, he staggered to his feet. Stefanie calmly got out of the car. She put her hands on her hips and looked at him as if she was angry he'd stood up. She was not concerned about his welfare. She got back into the car and screeched off.

Later, Parker would believe he put himself behind the car (twice now) on purpose, hoping she'd put him out of his misery.

★ ★ ★

The next day, Ramsey met Parker at the Rookery office. Ramsey had been instructed to check on Parker's mental state, since many of the conversations and incidents with his wife were listened to by NSA officials.

"Look, Parker, what's going on with your wife?" Ramsey was sincere.

"I don't know—No, that's not true. I do know; I just don't know what to do. There is so much drama in my life ... at least I know where I live. I think my wife's crazy. Actually, I know she's crazy, but I wasn't prepared for that. Never saw it coming. I guess I see it as my lot in life. The busier I am with work and the more time I spend with the kids, well, it keeps me out of harm's way, except then I have to hope and pray she doesn't go ballistic when we get together." Parker had difficulty maintaining eye contact with Ramsey.

"Parker, you're rambling. You're the expert. I'm just saying ..."

Parker cut him off. "What you're saying is what everyone I know is starting to ask. I don't know what to do right now. Okay?" He was yelling.

Ramsey just shook his head and got to work setting up Parker's device.

"Chatter about the FBI is getting close. We may have to finally get you out of here."

"Anytime Ramsey. Anytime."

★   ★   ★

He was trying to drive from Chicago to Michigan, oftentimes daily, to make sure he saw George play hockey and his daughter, Julie, play soccer. He loved keeping score at his son's high school games, especially since George had been made captain. Each time Parker attended one of his children's events, Stefanie's abuse worsened. Once he attended one of Julie's games wearing a tweed sport coat. When he got home, Stefanie accused Parker of trying to pick up one of his daughter's teammates. The yelling that night went into the wee hours of the morning.

Chapter 30

It was August 2007, fourteen months before the 2008 election, the U.S. Senator from Illinois was at the Navy Pier for a dinner and speaking engagement. Ramsey met with Parker earlier that day at the Elephant and Castle Pub on Adams.

"Parker, you need to be on your game tonight. Let others talk and don't prattle on if you disagree. This will be an important night for us to get information." Ramsey was serious. "It seems things have settled at home, but you know your wife is out all the time with others? Did you know she was with your ex-labor executive last week, right here in Chicago? Play the game tonight and we'll work on steps to help get you out. This may be your last foray in Chicago and Illinois politics. Things are boiling in another state."

Parker listened. He was dressed in his best black suit, but he was depressed. His depression was becoming obvious to everyone—and his contract at work would be coming up in a couple months.

★　★　★

The Illinois senator made his way amongst the guests. It was curious to watch the new entourage of bodyguards surrounding him. There was an aura of change. There were standing ovations and a love affair between the audience and senator unlike any Parker had ever witnessed. The tension that typically hung in a room while waiting for the real message was nonexistent. The man held the people like clay on a potter's wheel; his voice was the moist hand that shaped their feelings. His eloquence offered comfort in what Parker had experienced as a crooked system. That night, Parker spent thousands on a dinner for fifteen Chicago voters of influence simply so they could listen and be listened to.

The evening allowed Parker to forget the violence at home. It made him forget the fact that at any given moment Stefanie could be with any given man for any given amount of money—but for purposes of his agreement, he stayed in the marriage. As his mind wandered back and forth, from the home front to what he had just experienced, he took some joy in watching the people around him enjoy their dinners and drinks while talking about a bright future. If he could only feel the same hope.

★   ★   ★

The night after the dinner, Parker was lying on the couch watching TV. He was home in Michigan. He had not been able to fall asleep; so he'd gotten out of bed. He heard footsteps coming down the stairs, then on the hardwood floor behind him.

"What the hell are you doing?" Stefanie's face was tight, eyes drawn, and hands on her hips as she bent over him.

"Uh, I was awake … couldn't get to sleep …" he replied.

"What the fuck is that about? When I'm in bed, you're supposed to be in bed," she said wild-eyed.

He knew it was time to get out. In some locales, domestic violence is almost equal between men and women as perpetrators. Both victims find it hard to leave, either for reasons of security or the everlasting desire to believe it will get better. As many an expert notes, there is security with the abuser knowing what's at hand.

Change brings fear of the unknown.

Chapter 31

Parker made many trips to D.C. He would routinely meet Agent Brooks on a bench across the street from the Smithsonian's red-brick visitors' center. With the great monuments to America nearby, this was one of Parker's favorite areas. Somehow it allowed him to believe in the system he was working in. Knowing there was a central togetherness that made for a great nation kept him afloat.

This time, however, Brooks visited Parker in his hotel room at the L'Enfant Plaza Hotel on the L'Enfant Plaza SW near the Capitol. Brooks was dressed as a maintenance worker for the hotel. Parker knew that for Brooks to take this kind of a risk meant something was changing.

"Parker, you've done great work. We have enough on the systems in Illinois and Michigan to bag some bad guys. One governor will go down and some economic chips will soon fall. We even have information on the greatest Ponzi scheme ever hatched related to some lobby visits you taped for us in Springfield and D.C. But …"

Parker wanted to concentrate on what Brooks was saying, but he couldn't. He was exhausted. He was brittle. His happiness and compassion for a cause were eroding at an alarming rate. Now he wasn't sure if he was becoming bipolar or taking on the horrible personality traits of his wife. His single-malt friends, Lagavulin and Talisker, were becoming nightly companions.

"… we're not done with you. You're going to resign from your job in Chicago and await the next assignment. No offense, Parker, but you look like shit. If your organization renews your contract, it will be a miracle. Let us get you away for a while. We're setting the scenario, but I can't tell you where yet."

"Maybe Antarctica?" Parker sat with his shoulders slumped.

"I will tell you, the potential for internal destruction to our country's energy policy is right around the corner. We need you on the inside."

"I don't do energy," Parker said.

"No, but you can get close to everybody. You will hear all about national and foreign influences that shape the price of crude through influence-lobbying, hedge funds, traders, and the oil companies. You and many others are getting to the root of how the wealth-divide in this country continues to be the growing threat. Here's your resignation letter. Just e-mail it. Leave a copy on your desk and disappear. We'll take care of the rest." Brooks left.

Parker was breathless. He paced in his room then decided to make his regular rounds at the Smithsonian. He visited the exhibits his kids loved best: the great blue whale, the space capsules, and planes. He then went to the monuments where heroes were honored, which always brought a respectful tear to his eye. He wasn't a hero anymore, at least not one anyone would recognize.

Chapter 32

Parker followed orders and cleaned out his office in Chicago without causing any interest in his coworkers. He and Dick barely talked anymore. He packed quietly and carried several loads of boxes to his car. He checked his e-mails, and again noticed one or two marked as previously opened. Before he walked out of the office for the last time, he hit the send button on the last e-mail. A copy of his resignation letter was on his desk too. He didn't call home because he would be crucified for dropping such an income. He knew that would not be the emotional release he needed.

Parker was in his car, driving through Indiana. His cell phone rang.

"Parker, you all right?" It was Dick.

"No. I will be, but right now, no."

"What should I do?"

"Keep the fort. They'll appoint a new CEO, and you can keep working. You are more indispensable than I."

"Parker, this place won't work the same."

"Dick, I'm about cooked. I can't even imagine what my night is going to be like. I'll call in a couple of days. I'm sorry." Parker clicked off.

When he arrived home, he was lucky. There were no kids about and she was gone. Ramsey phoned soon after Parker walked through the door. He didn't identify himself as Ramsey, but Parker recognized the voice.

"Mr. Moore? This is Ed Baxter at Joliet General Hospital. We've met before. We'd like to hire you for some consulting work with our administrators. Mostly HR stuff, like keeping the unions happy and maybe preventing some trouble down the road. If you're up for it, we'd like you down here next week."

"Well, sure. Let me set some time aside and make arrangements …" Ramsey interrupted him. Parker recognized the phone number of the hospital. How was Ramsey pulling that off?

"Don't worry, Mr. Moore. Everything has been arranged. Your flight leaves from Lansing on Thursday of next week. You'll fly into Midway and a car will be waiting. We'll meet in a small restaurant away from town so we can talk. We want to discuss if we should get rid of one of our leaders; so we'd like to do that away from here. A courier will deliver your tickets and itinerary tomorrow. Have a good day, Mr. Moore."

The phone call ended. Parker grabbed a snifter of Macallen 16 and walked out to the bench to watch the sunset. The bench faced west and was surrounded by the roses Parker planted two years ago.

Parker was at the end of his rope. If it wasn't for the fishing trips with Nelson and George and the visits with Julie, he would have driven his car off a cliff. He was getting more reckless. He drove faster. He drank more. The sex was hard and often violent. His kayaking and mountain-bike rides became more dangerous—it was all a release. He never used drugs, but the adrenalin rush he got from everything else was no different. He could go weeks on three hours of sleep a night; then he went months. He had days when he couldn't get out of bed. He was always smiling for show. His private times were deeper and deeper into despair—he had enough insight to know he was becoming impaired.

"So, when were you going to tell me?" Stefanie was her usual wild self. Keys banged on the counter. Heels echoed loud on the hardwood floor.

"Tell you what?" Parker was always timing when he could talk to Stefanie to prepare for the onslaught; his reply was a delay. He never could reach a consistency with the abuse, and at times chose it before rather than after the situation. On this day, he needed a delay.

"About you quitting. What are we going to do for money?"

"How did you find out?"

"I got a call." Stefanie's angry affect suddenly changed. The ever-present brain switch. She looked outside and became busy on her phone–deleting calls.

Parker didn't say a word. He now knew who was getting into his e-mails. At sometimes four hundred of them a day, no wonder she mistakenly left a few marked as already opened. He wasn't sure about a call. He became preoccupied and lost track of Stefanie.

The fact that the NSA was sending him to a new assignment was a godsend. It was that or a convenient car crash into an embankment late at night. Parker had become like the people he was always trying to fix.

"FUCK!" she yelled as she came downstairs.

"Stefanie, we'll be fine. I have several offers." Parker was jolted out of his thoughts.

"Yeah, whatever. I'm going out." She left.

Parker was finally realizing there was no emotional attachment. *Where did she come from? How did she get into my life? And why?*

"What the hell is happening around me?" Parker softly said to himself as he walked back outside to the rose garden.

★   ★   ★

She was in her car driving down Grand River toward Lansing. Her cell phone rang for the tenth time when she finally looked at it and realized it wasn't Parker. She picked it up.

"Did he make it home?" It was Peabody.

"Of course. I couldn't be so lucky. How much longer will you be sending me money?"

"Why? He's not our problem anymore."

"So, all the money at once, gone?"

"I guess so."

"You know, I have plenty of takers. I'll just take my pick and be done with it." She hit the end button and turned up the Dave Matthews band.

In Springfield, Peabody set down his cell phone and shook his head. He almost felt sorry for Parker Moore.

Chapter 33

The restaurant was in Tinley Park, a small town between the Southside of Chicago and Joliet. Parker was aware of his entitlements and used them to his advantage. He was an influence peddler like the rest—although inside it ate him alive. He always got the best table and the most expensive scotch. Today it was Lagavulin.

"Mr. Moore, it's nice to see you again," said Ramsey as he stuck out his hand.

"Yes. Mr. Baxter, is it? What can I do for you?" The two men sat down and scanned the room to see who was in the restaurant. Parker was a public figure in Illinois and this seemed chancy.

"Don't worry, Parker. Everyone in here belongs to us. Parker, you're going to Alaska."

"What? Everyone? Even the chef? I hope he can cook." Parker's sarcasm was healthy at the moment. There was still stress in his life but he didn't have the political drama of Illinois and Chicago. Parker was born in Alaska and for many years took his family there for six weeks at a time in the motor home. The adventures could make movies, and the kids loved the trips. "I can do Alaska."

"We have issues with their new governor and some influence-shaping that's going to send oil prices skyrocketing. We need a person totally away from that side of the fence but close enough for us to get what we need. Recently they've had state legislators tagged for bribery and money laundering, but it's not stopping. It's mostly for public show. The real trouble is coming from Canadian oil companies and the new China markets. The people we're watching have influenced the state elections and gotten a governor elected who they plan on using for far greater influence beyond Alaska. The Senator from Illinois you heard speak at the Navy Pier, the Super PAC, and our agency need to be ready for whatever comes next. If what we think may happen happens, well …"

Parker was in survival mode. The abuse had worsened and he rarely spent a night not locked in a room away from her. He was also tired of taking the public hits for the NSA's needs. At fifty, he was blackballed anywhere the government didn't need him. He could not continue to do this forever.

"Parker? Are you listening?" Ramsey grabbed Parker by the forearm. "You'll take another union job, but you will spend most of your time in Juneau. You'll be set up with another multi-client lobby firm and begin feeding us information."

"I want this to be the last one," Parker said. "I don't care what happens. I don't care what you do to me. I want out after this. I want peace and quiet. I want out of the marriage and out of my life." Parker was not doing a good job of staying in cover. He was angry and getting loud. "Do you hear me?" he shouted.

"Mr. Moore, please," Ramsey said with a smile as he looked around the quiet restaurant.

"I'm not fooling around." Parker's big frame came out of the chair and he leaned across the table.

"Parker, in about five seconds you're gonna be on the ground and never see the light of day. Now, you've got a place to be, and that's it. End of discussion." Ramsey had never pulled the federal trump card on Parker, but had done so with many people in other states who were doing what Parker was. Certain officials in the Justice Department were connected to the group and were keeping threats over people's heads. "By the way, we've expanded our net and found your wife in your e-mail and taking calls from Peabody, the governor's advisor."

"No shit; that's old news." Parker sat back in his chair. He didn't know about the calls. "Send me the details and get me the hell out of Michigan."

He got up and left.

Chapter 34

Parker drove the rental car back to Midway. He went deep into thought while waiting for his plane.

The energy he felt was new and yet old. Like a spiritual awakening, the last ten years of his professional life were coming to light as fast as he could think. He had brought the latest quotes from the *Chicago Tribune* that were attributed to him to read. They weren't even close to the truth. The reporters were overtly more interested in the ability to sell themselves, their stations, or their newspaper. Any sensationalism in wording or picture was the actual story.

What the average Joe on the street didn't realize was how he or she was being led by the nose into someone else's agenda on an almost daily basis. Regardless of the source—radio, newspapers, Internet—people received a diatribe of conjecture, half-truths and media manipulation so those in public office could continue their jobs, those who could afford the manipulation could retain their wealth, and those who wanted both did whatever they could to stir the pot.

It started by buying a voice. Parker knew from his own small business how easy it was to grow once he placed himself in the right circles. He also learned that his ability to carry a debate and discussion without stammering or appearing flummoxed made him a valuable commodity to whoever wanted to pay him.

He took the jobs as they came, from groups that wanted to advance or win affiliation with others. Parker succeeded at both. Everyone got bigger, richer, or more powerful. They enjoyed the limelight together. The problem for Parker was that everyone he helped placed him in a situation of gaining political enemies or being blackballed for entry into further work down the road. Parker learned that his addiction to the inside game of politics placed him at a moral compass point he didn't realize until too late. It had two red arrows pointing south. Board members of associations and advocacy groups, and all sides of the current political forces, conservative and liberal, Republican and Democrat, union and non-union wanted the same thing: all the power and all the wealth. Entitlements and money flowed so easily that most lost track of what principle they were supposed to be fighting for. Politicians became so wealthy doing politics they had to keep working to hold onto their jobs, which happened by collecting campaign funds from as many groups and as many people as possible and giving the biggest ear to the largest contributors. There were no heroes. All elected politicians had to play that game or they lost their job.

Any time Parker needed to carry forth an argument for legislation or some rule or statute interpretation, he watered the earth with dinners, drinks, and campaign donations. He made nice gestures by mentioning House members or senators in a speech, lecture, or press release. The boards that employed him for change never realized the work of putting hundreds, if not thousands, of opinions together; arranging testimony, putting the right constituents together with their elected officials, and making sure everyone was happy so a favorable outcome would be reached for those who wanted more power and influence.

Businesses employed people like Parker to improve their ability to obtain greater influence and thus pave the way for shareholders to capitalize on profit and dividends, oftentimes through federal contracts–going to the same people that complained bitterly about federal entitlements. On the for-profit health-care front it meant leverage with insurance companies, health-care systems, or government-sponsored programs. If nonprofits or associations wanted influence, the game was the same. It generally involved less money but greater tugs on the heartstrings. The more public the heartstring the better, as that placed pressure on legislators and officials the same as money. The best politicians didn't mind a little negative public opinion from time to time because they knew how short people's memories were. If enough businesses were in their corner, their donations would work to get them elected anyway.

The entire system of government had always heavily favored the wealthy, and now that wealth was worldwide. The days of Lincoln keeping the British out of the Civil War by writing the Emancipation Proclamation were long past. Brilliant strategic thinking had been replaced by large amounts of money that flowed through businesses that wished to gain influence in the United States and, on the flip side, by unions and advocacy groups that wanted the same power for their agendas. The winners in this new-world structure were the banks, Wall Street gamblers, fund manipulators, and politicians who could win the public eye in the media. The system was set up so ingeniously that everyone's retirement fund actually provided the income to keep the scheme going; thus the top-secret program of the NSA. It wasn't only American companies buying influence. Now very wealthy individuals and companies from around the world were buying America, to the point that the U.S. economic and social infrastructures were at risk. When Parker shook the hand of that Illinois Senator, they looked at each other with a trust few find at a first meeting; he felt a comfort. He felt a knowledge that no matter what happened to him, eventually he'd find peace. Parker didn't know the Senator knew he was wearing a wire.

Parker was sick and tired of being sick and tired. He faced abusive board members, abusive politicians, and an abusive wife. He was a part of the dirty secrets at work and at home. He needed out. The NSA's top-secret program of investigating the corrupt political system gave him the out for which he'd been praying.

Parker's plane was at the gate, but he remained sitting. He always figured the plane wasn't going anywhere until everyone walked on, and that was after the ten times they'd ask for final boarding. He watched everyone talking on their phones and reading papers as they stood in line waiting to board.

He looked over at the coffee shop behind the gate; there she was. The twin to his wife complete with the heels and dark sunglasses. She didn't even try to avert her glance. Actually, she smiled and waved at him.

Parker just stared.

She returned the stare.

As he finally walked up to the gangway, he looked back toward the coffee shop while the attendant checked his ticket.

"Thank you, Mr. Moore. Have a nice flight."

Parker watched the woman walk away as he went further down the gangway. He felt like he was walking the plank into an unknown sea. He turned and smiled. Whoever all these people were, they were out of his mind the instant he sat down.

Chapter 35

Back to the Middle
Michigan—2010

Parker knew he was in a hospital, but wasn't sure where or why. No memory of the shooting; only a continuous review of the past. When he awoke it was for brief periods and he kept his eyes closed. He listened. Sometimes he heard people talking and sometimes he only heard the beeps and slurs of the equipment that was helping him stay alive.

★　★　★

The only thing she gave any thought to was when she tossed the gun into the river. The snow banks were high and she wasn't sure where it landed, but she heard a splash. The Boyne Mountain Resort was where she liked to go for all seasons; so the river in Boyne Falls was a known convenience she took advantage of before continuing south.

She pulled off U.S. 127 South onto Michigan Avenue. She passed her office building, where she played the innocent, and headed down Grand River past the Meridian Mall. Before going home, she'd make a quick stop at Victoria's Secret. Anything she ever needed was just a striptease away.

Blair was in bed sleeping. Dinner was on the table. She only needed to zap it in the microwave. She smiled as she ate spaghetti and looked out the back windows into the dark expanse of the estate. This one will do the trick. No one can survive that shot. She began to hum, put down her fork, and grabbed the wine glass by its stem. She held it up as she examined the color of the pinot in the candlelight, stuck her nose into the glass to sniff, and remembered how she had learned. A long way from Coors Lite. A long way from doors that didn't work and landscapes that looked like no one cared. It started on a hill near a little league field. The fool.

★   ★   ★

"What the hell? You come home late, eat, sleep, and now you're screaming at me?" Blair was up early, expecting everything was going to be okay—but Venus had turned to Sybil.

"Screaming? Screaming? All I want is for you to tell me why you went to bed last night before I got home. You know I hate that." Stefanie was yelling at the top of her lungs.

"Really? You were out somewhere, doing something that I will never know because you never talk except to demand. Shopping or getting drunk. That's when you're happy!"

As she began to shove him, he turned and his glasses flew toward the stove. He gathered himself and began to walk toward her.

"You touch me, I'll have your ass in jail so fast your head will spin!" she said, praying he'd do it.

Blair pushed her from behind on her left shoulder as she pretended to run away. Pretending, because she had no intention of moving. She hit the floor face down landing mostly with her palms, forearms, and knees taking the shock.

He did it. The moron actually did it, she thought. She lay quiet for a few seconds. Blair was several feet behind her, breathing heavily and staring down with his hands on his knees.

"Are you all right?" he asked.

Silence.

"Hey? You okay? I'm sorry."

She stood and bolted upstairs. A door slammed.

Chapter 36

Okemos was built on the outskirts of Lansing to house the overflow of automotive executives, association management professionals, political insiders, and university and government employees. New subdivisions, schools, shops, and strip malls made for a comfortable existence through avoidance of anything real. No one cared how they got there; it was just about arriving. It was about how much you could get and how much you could flaunt it.

The chilliness of the estate was the norm for this town. All brick with a manicured landscape maintained by the lawn service that employed illegals while the estate owner voted for politicians who wanted to end illegal immigration. There were granite kitchen countertops and the space allotted for Saturday football games on the big screen in the media room. Relationships weren't built on spiritual connections or the interweaving of time and family, they were built on shallow need for survival of the wealthiest. The new entitled bottom of Maslow's pyramid, not the top, formed the structure of this neighborhood.

Soccer games and cocktail parties in between jet trips to places that only kept the appearances up and the egos connected to the greater pages of *People* magazine were standard. Dyed hair, whitened teeth, and an avoidance of all spiritual depth provided a trip to a nirvana not found in the recesses of the brain but only in the first layer of the frontal lobe.

★   ★   ★

The sheriff's deputies arrived in two cars. They walked past the flowers tended by the landscaping service and up to the vaulted entryway. She sat on the bed looking at her nails. The French manicure was fading and needed touching up. She wondered what to get the kids for their birthdays. The bedroom door was locked; all she kept hearing was the same thing over and over again.

"Look, I'm sorry. Will you please let me in? We'll do what you always like to do to make up. The kids are gone."

The pounding on the door was getting louder. Suddenly the door crashed open. After the scream, the officers rushed into the house.

"Police!"

She punched Blair in the gut as she flew by him. As he reached for her, she threw herself down the stairs in a head-first slide that made Chet Lemon famous for diving into first base. The startled deputies yanked their weapons and looked wide-eyed to see the blonde hair draped over the head of a woman in a tank top and the newest version of a Victoria's Secret thong. She was silent for a moment then screamed, "Get him the fuck outta here!"

She got to her hands while leaning on one knee and still not looking up. Her knees were bloody, and no one could see the smile come over her face. Those shouldn't scar. Who cares? The money she'd make in the divorce would pay for plastic surgery if needed.

"Who's upstairs, ma'am?"

"Who else, but another asshole."

Blair rounded the upstairs corner and was slowly moving down the stairs in disbelief. *This can't be happening,* he thought. *This is like a nightmare you read about in books or watch on TV.*

"Sir, please stand still."

Blair froze as he stared at the figure at the bottom of the stairs.

The hair that would flow over him in times of passion. The legs that would run down the beach toward him. The jewelry he bought her just to see her smile.

He was cuffed and led past her and out the door. Nothing was said. All was silent.

As the sheriff deputy drove Blair to the police station, he remembered the woman. It would have been ten years ago, but he remembered arresting her husband. It wasn't this guy. This guy said he was her third husband and that it was her fault. The deputy wondered what happened to husband number two.

Blair sat in the backseat behind bars. He thought about his job and his standing with his clients. More anger than sadness began to boil. *What a dupe.*

Chapter 37

"Dad? Dad? Can you hear me?"

Sounded like Julie. She was the daughter every man wanted. Twenty-five, beautiful, gifted, amazing intelligence, soft, and finishing graduate school.

"Are you okay? We're all here, Dad. We love you."

Parker could only look through a haze and smile. He nodded his head. *I'm here, Julie. I'm here.* Nobody could hear him, but he thought the words as loud as he could.

"You're through surgery, and it will be okay," Julie said a few times as she peered down at her father. She was practically yelling.

"Dad, we have to go fishing next week, so get your ass outta this bed. Now!" said George, his middle son who was home from law school.

"Hey, Dad? Do you really think we're gonna let you lay there and sleep? You've been waking us up for years in the middle of the night with stupid movie quotes and game scores." Nelson's eyes teared as he talked, but he knew his dad would be okay. Nelson was the youngest and a freshman at the University of Michigan.

"Okay, okay. I can hear you all. Kiss my ass." Parker was finally able to whisper a few words. His voice was raspy and low, but understood nonetheless. Everyone smiled and cried at the same time.

Sam stood behind his children. She was holding her hands over her cheeks as she listened and watched. The shock of the last two days hadn't subsided. No sleep. No food. Only a constant vigil. *Why would someone, anyone, do this? What driving force would lead someone to such an act of violence?* Sam had experienced her own violence many years ago; having to face it all again was surreal. Sam knew there were issues she didn't always understand when Parker would get quiet and weep softly while he rebuilt his life. She remembered those discussions and journal entries hinting at abuse and confusion living with a borderline, the political enemies, and his life being threatened by several people. His public and political crucifixions were all in the past—until the shattered glass, the rushing in of police, EMTs, and firemen. No matter how much she turned to her past as a lieutenant in the fire service, this was different. Parker was connected to her. What she respected was how fast his children arrived and how well they handled the situation. Polite, steadfast, and with nothing but hope. Always a constant, positive hope.

Parker felt Sam squeezing his hand as he drifted off to the past once again.

Chapter 38

Back to the Beginning
Michigan, Illinois, Washington D.C., and Alaska—2007-2008

In the fall of 2007, Parker made final arrangements to leave Michigan. There was a small family party to send him off. His brother asked privately if this was Parker's chance to finally leave Stefanie. Parker only smiled and said nothing. He knew about the multiple affairs. He didn't know who they were with, but in true borderline fashion, her reaction was to be tearful and angry about his departure. Parker actually, as sick as it was, believed maybe she'd soon follow him to Alaska and the kids could come back and forth for a wonderful experience. She could take a leave of absence for up to a year, but he later learned she had no intention of leaving. What Parker didn't know, nor did the agents, was that one of the men she was seeing was making long-term plans for to move all of the furniture Parker had purchased into her new house.

Parker and Stefanie arrived at the Ted Steven's Airport in Anchorage late on a Thursday. She came along as a way to get a free trip to Alaska and to make sure she could control the moving advance Parker received with his contract. She ended up keeping half of it.

They drove to the downtown Hilton on Third Avenue and checked in. After a night's sleep, they bought Parker a car, found an apartment to rent over a garage in a nice neighborhood called Rogers Park, went grocery shopping, and introduced themselves to the union members at a cocktail gathering. As usual, everyone was enamored with Stefanie. The striking features, height, and heels, along with her choice of tight designer jeans and jacket kept everyone very interested. For added spark, she made sure the back strap of her silver G-string flashed out of her jeans whenever she had to bend over. Parker just made the rounds, shaking hands and talking about his past adventures in Alaska. To any outsider, all seemed as it should.

On her last day in Anchorage, Stefanie made sure Parker wouldn't forget her. The night was long and voracious, but the next morning, Parker's gut was screaming. His jaws were tight, and he was beginning to experience new physical symptoms. She whistled and sang all the way to the airport.

Once her plane took off, Parker sat in the airport and didn't know what to do next. On one hand he was relieved, yet there was a fear he'd never felt before.

Chapter 39

Back in his birthplace, Parker felt like he was home. People dressed like him, enjoyed the same outdoor activities, and the weather was always cool. He liked Anchorage.

It was a Monday morning in October. On his way to the office, Parker noticed a car following him. He knew the routine well enough to visit the first local coffee shop he could find; so he drove to the Snow City Café at 4th and L Street. He ordered a black coffee and the man who was following him did the same. It was a nice day, so they sat outside on the picnic table facing L Street. The ocean air was strong with salt; Anchorage breezes always carried the odor of willow.

"I didn't expect to see you here," Parker said to Brooks.

"Me either. I wanted to give you some details," Brooks replied.

Just then a young couple walked by, and the conversation at the picnic table stopped abruptly. Both men sipped their coffee. Parker smiled and thought of Burger and Victor Laszlo sitting at the bar at Rick's American Café drinking champagne cocktails waiting for the bartender to leave so they could discuss the whereabouts of Ugarte.

"Of all the gin joints in all the towns in all the world, you walk into mine," said Parker. He couldn't help himself. Being in Anchorage and away from the torment of abuse, he felt half human.

His moods were as quick to switch now as hers. He couldn't tell who the borderline was anymore.

Brooks didn't smile. Parker realized he probably didn't recognize the quote.

"You'll have a contact here with the central AFL/CIO office. He'll find you. The first step is to get you wired and start taking notes at your union office. We have nothing on them yet, other than the second-largest hospital system in the Northwest wants the union gone.

"In Juneau, the governor is already in trouble. The conservatives that put her in office are turning on her. They never really liked her, but the people in Alaska are different. It's still the Wild West in some respects and people love to be different. It's their claim to fame. Trouble for the governor is there's mounting tension to move the oil leases and there are billions involved—for everyone. She actually acted like a Democrat and gave money to the Native groups living in the bush. Conservatives don't like entitlements. What's worse is we know she's being asked to consider higher office in the upcoming elections. She has the looks and balls to gain public support wherever she goes. If the wealth of the oil and the national elections connect, we haven't gained anything in our attempts to change the system, and there are very wealthy people behind her."

Parker listened. His work in Michigan and Illinois involved small time stuff compared to this. As he listened, Brooks talked about the Chinese, Canadian, and Japanese influence around the oil. The oil companies and speculators could soon become the power behind higher oil and gas prices. If the Alaska governor did as she was directed, the wealthy would gain beyond belief. It would look as if she's being heroic for the Greenpeace types and other environmentalists—however, that bought into the hand of big oil and the speculators. Prices and profits would skyrocket while the average consumer went broke. People in Alaska already paid the highest gas prices in the country because the oil didn't turn into gas until it went somewhere else and came back. They did reap the benefits of yearly payoffs for living there, and they paid no taxes. The cost of living was high, but people had the money to spend.

Brooks didn't waste much time. The conversation ended, and he walked around the corner and was gone.

Parker sat and closed his eyes. The sun was gone and it began to drizzle, but he didn't move.

What next?

Chapter 40

The first meeting with Vic was at New Sagaya's on 13th Street. It was a natural food store which meant it was full of really expensive, hard-to-find food. There was a picnic table out front; the fall sun was out again.

"Where are you staying?" asked Vic.

"A mother-in-law apartment over a garage in Rogers Park. Nice older woman needs some extra cash," Parker replied.

"Give me the address, and I'll be around tomorrow after midnight. I assume you have an alley entry?"

"Yup."

"Good. I also assume you know the setup with the wire. Once on, I'll contact you when we need to meet. Just do your thing. The local flights don't have any detectors or checks, so you'll have no problem flying around the state. On your trips to D.C., we'll set you free and meet you on arrival."

Vic explained things clearly. He was a couple inches shorter than Parker, and thicker and balding. He carried the look of the North Slope places he used to work for the DEA. His claim to fame in Prudhoe Bay was helping to bust a massive drug ring that had pipeline workers so high the thing looked like a sieve between the Slope all the way to Valdez. He was on loan to NSA to handle Parker. Brooks and Ramsey figured if anything got heavy, Vic would be a good guy to have around.

Chapter 41

"**Hello, Parker.** It's nice to have you here." said Diane, the local union president.

"Thank you. It's nice to be here." Parker walked in dressed in a shirt and tie carrying his favorite briefcase.

"We're all putting in time today." She looked around and leaned toward Parker. "We called in." She laughed.

On his first day at work, Parker found three union board executives in the office..

"We hate the people we work for. One of your first jobs is to try and get them fired." Diane's whisper was loud. She looked at the others and smiled as they walked into the back conference room. The windows allowed for a breathtaking view of the Chugach Mountains.

The trio explained their hate for their supervisors at the hospital; all three were earning sick time pay plus getting union pay for being at the office. Parker just listened, acted nice, and realized this was worse than Chicago. At least in Chicago, everyone knew the history and expectations of crooked politicians, unions, and political machines, but the union members didn't come into the office to work and get paid by both jobs.

"You pay yourself for working here after you call in sick at the hospital and get paid for that?" Parker said.

"It's Alaska, Parker. We do what we want. It's different up here," said Diane.

Grace, who only worked at her hospital job about one day a week, added, "Our job is to make that hospital pay with blood. Now that you're here, will never lose."

The women chuckled.

In Anchorage, Parker wasn't sure what he'd find. In his dual role as executive and lobbyist, the NSA seemed more interested in the oil stuff, but he knew one was connected to the other. Influence was influence. Unions wanted the oil leases opened up for more members to work and pay dues. His mind was wandering.

"This hospital makes so much money and gives us so little," added Sherry, the third member.

"How much do you all make?" Parker asked.

"Diane makes around forty an hour; Grace about thirty-five; and me, around forty-five. Higher seniority." Sherry was open, knowing Parker would soon know the salary schedule.

"That's not bad. There are people in other parts of the country not making half of that who have more education hung on the wall."

"Trust us," Diane said, "this hospital system makes *billions*. We're a drop in the bucket."

Health-care systems grew anywhere there were people, and they didn't want the unions taking their profits. Parker always smiled when he thought about profits in health care. The profits in nonprofit religious-based hospital systems were called Revenues over Expenses, but they were profits, and administrators made millions now that the nuns and priests were gone. It was known as a mission with a margin.

"As union members, how do you feel about your governor?" Parker was curious about everything these women thought. He might as well give the NSA as much as he could.

"She's great. We all vote for her," Sherry said with a smile.

"How do you vote Republican if they want you and your union members to disappear?" Parker couldn't resist the prospect of the debate. He was going home to peace; no violence.

"So? She said she'd take good care of us. We're telling you, Parker. Alaska is different." Grace sat back in her chair and held her arms out and looked around the room as if to encompass the entire Last Frontier.

It was clear the governor was going to be at odds with these union folks. Another note Parker made was that the board members of the health-care union he was at were all conservative Republicans. That was a switch. So, were the hospital executives. This was going to be interesting.

"Okay. I'm going into my office and settle in. If you need anything, let me know." Parker got up and walked over to his office door. His view of the mountains was the same. He sat at his desk and just took in the scenery.

Later that evening, Parker walked through the Fred Meyer to purchase some milk and bread. He noticed moms and kids shopping, and some older Natives he'd seen drunk on 4th Avenue earlier. Parker's father used to tell stories of the guys from Fort Richardson who would accept the challenge of drinking at every bar down 4th. They usually got carried back to the barracks. Parker's attention suddenly turned to a couple outside the state liquor store within the Fred Meyer. They were commenting about the gas prices going up and swearing at BP and Chevron as they pointed to the nearby high-rise offices of the Native corporations. The public was angry, but the new governor was their hero. She'd show 'em.

After returning to his apartment, he lay on the couch falling asleep waiting for Vic. There was a knock on the door. Vic was standing on the top step looking around. Parker let him in.

"How was your first day?" asked Vic.

"Revealing."

"If you don't mind, I'd like to get this set and get the hell outta here. I did some investigation on this place. It's out of code and the old lady never filed the proper papers for inspections or alterations. She also rents out a house around the corner that's been busted for drugs countless times. She's just a landlord, but the neighborhood is watching this place to make sure she doesn't rent to the same lowlifes. It doesn't matter what you do or who you are, they want this garage apartment shut. Start looking for a new place." Vic wasn't playing around. He knew deep cover and this was the last place he wanted someone he was handling.

"Okay. Wow. I'll get right on it." Parker was sarcastic and annoyed. He took a sip of some warm Alaskan Amber beer left in the bottle he was drinking before falling asleep.

Vic finished with the explanations and the mechanics of the wire. He placed some equipment around the garage and under Parker's silver Ford Fusion. Vic always prepared for the very worst.

★   ★   ★

Parker awoke with a start. He was sweating. He was having one of those dreams between reality and fear. He had heard the footsteps coming downstairs. He was in Michigan. He was lying in bed half asleep and she'd been out drinking with her softball team. Now she was in heels and jeans walking on the hardwood floors—a sound he heard all too often before she'd begin one of her tirades. Then she'd demand sex. A demand that most men would envy. Until the violence began. Never an apology. This dream was different, though. She came up the stairs and when he turned over he was looking at a nickel-plated .357. That's when he woke up.

Chapter 42

After the first few months, his routine was steady. Parker won all the grievances the union filed. He even cleaned up a couple arbitrations while gaining friendships with a few of the attorneys in town. There was newfound energy in organizing and Parker was sure he'd claim his first victory on the Kenai. The hospitals already hated him, but they continued to buy him dinner. The legislature was just getting heated up, so he made a few trips to Juneau where he met his multi-client lobby firm of Mitch, Sara, and Mike. Mitch was a retired state administrator who had contracts with several communities as far away as Bethel. Whether it was a Yup'ik or an Athabaskan community, Mitch was a good person for them to have in Juneau. He also had quiet connections to oil groups and the greatest influence in his lobby firm—it was a perfect place to get to know everyone connected to the state government.

It didn't take long for Parker to observe how the governor and the state legislators worked. Juneau was different than Illinois and Michigan. Much more informal. Not everyone wore business suits, and you dressed for the weather. Parker got used to wearing his black suit for hearing days with his Merrill's. As the NSA predicted, soon Parker was a star. He was on the news and in the newspapers, and making inroads where he was supposed to. There was more damning information on the union he worked for: expensive plane tickets, frequent air miles for personal use, sick time and union pay on the same day, and bringing relatives along on junkets. Nothing big, but what the NSA had overlooked was Parker's continued lapse into depression.

The geographical cure no longer provided comfort. As the days grew shorter, Parker stood in a gun store contemplating suicide. He was alone and all his money was going back to Michigan.

★   ★   ★

Several calls home and to her cell phone went unanswered. Parker was now sick with the flu and without health insurance. His contract didn't pay for any, and he thought he could get coverage as her spouse through her plan at the university. She didn't want to allow it. He begged and begged. After sending the last check home and having just enough left for gas, Parker made his first fatal error in his dissociative state: he used the union credit card to pay for the emergency room visit. He was sicker than he thought.

★   ★   ★

One night in Juneau, Parker was alone. He'd been successful at a Senate hearing and the hospitals were reeling. After a quiet dinner and some Lagavulin, Parker hit the sack at the Baranof. The Baranof was the hotel the FBI wired for years to trap several Alaskan legislators who were accepting bribes in return for favors. At about four in the morning, the phone rang.

"You got a fucking whore with you?" yelled Stefanie.

"What? What are you talking about?" Parker stammered awake. He sat up in bed trying to focus on something real in the room.

"We just heard your old friend, the senator from Michigan, found out her husband has been having affairs with hookers."

"You're crazy. I'm alone. We give her ten thousand dollars and I'm her friend? Why would you equate me with that news?"

"Because you're a man."

She hung up.

Parker wanted to scream into the phone. He slammed it down. His depression and suicidal ideation was turning to anger and homicidal ideation. He needed help.

The next day, he left for Anchorage and phoned his daughter.

Chapter 43

Julie arrived the day before the union vote on the Kenai. She was glad to see her dad, but he was happier to see her. Parker was working on instinct alone. He'd joined the local Catholic church; found a new apartment downtown, as Vic requested; and tried to keep his mind off the constant arguments he had with his wife. She had disappeared an entire night after a MSU football game a couple months ago. He knew what that meant, but it didn't do anything to clear his mind.

"Hey, Dad. Wow, you look awful," Julie said as she came through security at Ted Steven's Airport.

Parker's eyes were sullen, his hair was turning gray around the temples, and he had gained weight. He'd also added his single-malt scotch to his sleeping pills.

"Oh, Julie, you're a sight for sore eyes. We have a plane tomorrow for Kenai and a vote in Soldotna." Parker hugged her. He held her by the shoulders and looked at her eyes. "You're gonna save my life."

Julie had no idea what her dad was talking about.

Julie was in grad school and interested in labor law. The trip was planned by Parker to help her, but in reality, he needed a witness to the election and everyone else not connected to the hospital was busy. It was his only clear moment of thought to do something right for his oldest child and his members.

The trip was perfect. A unanimous vote brought a new unit in and another hospital enemy for Parker, but more money and influence for the union. Julie's visit helped Parker begin to sort his priorities. It wasn't his wife. It wasn't the crooked unions and politicians. It wasn't the NSA. It was his life with his three children. He had sold his soul while getting lost on the path of a very successful life.

Julie was asleep on the couch. Parker stared at his child and wrote in his journal. The moment wasn't clearing, but Parker had a glimmer of what he used to be. He'd read countless articles and books about failed executives, politicians, and lobbyists—people who lost track of their lives after getting used to entitlements and always playing the game. He was no different, not even with his undercover work for the NSA.

After a few days, Julie left. Parker sat at the lower bar in the Captain Cook Hotel. He was staring in the mirror and drinking a double pour of a Macallan 16. The taste was smoother than the usual Lagavulin, but the effects immediate. His phone vibrated in his pocket. He looked at the number and didn't answer. He couldn't bear the barrage.

Chapter 44

Parker made his decision. He was going to get out of this. He called domestic violence groups in Alaska. They only worked with women. They said they received lots of calls from men, but didn't know what to do with them. Parker called a psychologist who was listed in the yellow pages. Darryl Saunders was able to see him the next day.

After Parker described what was going on in his life, Dr. Saunders was quick with advice.

"Parker, you've married a borderline personality. She won't change. Now you need to find your own life." After mere minutes, Saunders was firm in his opinion.

Parker spent an hour and a half with Dr. Saunders consciously not mentioning the NSA, the wire, his suicidal thoughts, or the lobby side of his life. He was sure how they were connected, and he now knew how sick he was keeping it out of the conversation. Making it worse was his belief that things would somehow work themselves out.

★   ★   ★

Parker made inroads into the state legislature working only one bill. He had several meetings with state senators and representatives who were very much in line with his group, but his group paid no money in campaign funds. It didn't have a PAC. Parker had lots of meetings and lots of nods, but no votes. The hospitals sent teams of lobbyists against Parker. Mitch was like any other multi-client lobbyist. He had to be careful not to jeopardize his other clients' legislative agendas, so he was being conservative in his approach.

One meeting Parker set up with a state senator included a member of his union who wore a two-carat diamond and made sure everyone saw it. She also wore enough makeup to re-paint the Golden Gate Bridge. The good senator greeted them as they entered his office, but after ten minutes he excused Parker. The union member had accepted several sexual comments from the senator as compliments; they shut the door as Parker left. An hour later, she showed up downstairs at the entry.

Chapter 45

After a debriefing with his clients in the Capitol entrance, Parker walked to his favorite Juneau hangout. He ordered a sandwich and a Coke at the Silverbow Inn before the noon-hour rush. There was a dining area off to the side that was usually reserved for busier times, but they knew Parker and allowed him an early entrance. He sat down in a booth to eat his lunch and read the *Empire*, Juneau's newspaper. Two gentlemen came in from another entrance that was usually closed. They sat near the front of the Inn and didn't see Parker behind a partition right next to them.

"Right. Here's how we're doing. The leases will be held up and we will make a public push for more refineries and more drilling all over the U.S., but in reality, we all know that's not going to happen."

The voice was right out of a British spy movie. Parker could envision two heads inches apart, while one man stared down at the table and the other talked into an ear. He could discern the voice as British. He stayed frozen. Silent. He placed his back flat against the wood behind the booth and puffed out his chest trying to expose the wire to the voices. He held his breath as much as he could.

"On your end, you claim victory about keeping the public and wilderness safe. In the end, prices keep going up. Our guys in New York speculate on the gas, making huge profits for all of us. This is, as you Anglo's would say, a no-brainer. Without the regulation and with our friends from Gulf Coast Oil everywhere we need them, we can keep this party going for years."

"What if who we need to do this gets gun-shy or begins to change course?" It was the other guy.

He was more cautious. Parker could sense it in his voice—a heavy Texas drawl.

"Right. There is nothing that's going to stop this. Our countries are fighting wars on two fronts, making speculation already working in our favor. If the ground doesn't break with a drill in our own backyards, we make more profit than if we were to actually do the work." There was pleading in his voice, as if he needed the other's influence. "Besides the Supreme Court is ours, and we've secured the House and Senate. Soon we will not have to hide. What we are doing will be quite legal."

"Okay. Okay. Just make sure this meeting never happened."

"Right. I don't even know your name."

Parker heard two chairs squeak against the wood floor as the men stood up. He peered around the corner to watch the two suited men walk past the front desk of the Inn and out to the street. He never saw them again in Juneau.

I sure hope they got that one. This is getting way out of my league, Parker thought to himself.

Chapter 46

The next day, Mitch and Parker were waiting for a meeting with the governor. Mitch was six-two and along with Parker's six-five frame they looked like parents sitting in elementary school chairs awaiting a teacher conference. Parker was more interested in asking Mitch about what he heard yesterday, but wasn't sure how to bring it up and where to go with it. He'd wait.

The governor's office was on the second floor of the Capitol building in Juneau. The halls were decorated with paintings depicting the history of Alaska and portraying a hearty soul of survival. The carpet was inlaid with midnight blue and gold, while the walls were paneled with natural woods from the Southeast Panhandle of Alaska making for an ornate setting when compared with the rest of the old building.

"So, where's the governor?" Parker asked.

"Who knows?" Mitch started. "Lately she dashes from room to room or stays hidden behind other people so you barely ever know she's there."

"Her car is parked where it always is . . . and there's her personal bodyguard ... why in the hell is he always staring at me?"

"Maybe he likes you." Mitch smiled and looked at Parker. They were shoulder to shoulder. "They probably know your history with governors."

"Why can't we cross into one of those offices and wait?"

"See your boyfriend gazing at you? He won't let us. They've become very protective." Mitch had his head bent toward Parker and was whispering. "My God, he really won't take his eyes off you."

Parker was so conscious of his wire; his affect probably gave a hint to the well-trained bodyguard that something was amiss.

"Wait. Here comes somebody," Mitch said as he stood up.

Mitch wore a gray sport coat with shirt and tie, while Parker had on his best black suit.

"Gentlemen, please, this way." A short, pretty, young woman in a blue dress and black heels pointed with her left arm toward a conference room. "The governor's Chief of Staff will be in shortly."

Parker allowed Mitch to lead him down the hall past the bodyguard at his pedestal desk. He smiled at the guard as he walked by, and the guard nodded in response, then immediately turned back toward the glass doors leading into the Governor's Hall. Maybe he wasn't worried about Parker. Maybe it was just where he was sitting by the doors. In either case, Parker couldn't take his eye off the guard and was preoccupied as he walked.

Suddenly a door opened to Parker's right. It glanced against his shoulder.

"Oh, excuse me. Hi. Sorry." It was the governor.

She was slumped over slightly and wore a large brown vest. She was smaller than what Parker would have guessed. She averted eye contact with Parker and ducked immediately into another door just a few feet away. For all Parker knew it was a broom closet.

He only had a chance to nod.

"Come on, Parker. Don't linger. They're really nervous about people loitering in the hallway."

"I'm right here. Don't worry. Why are we whispering?" Parker followed Mitch into the conference room.

Sheila, the Governor's Chief of Staff, rushed into the room with an armful of papers and plopped them on the table at the same time she plopped down into a wooden chair. She took a deep breath. The kind where her cheeks puffed up and out then exhaled through pursed lips.

"Hello, Mitch. You must be Mr. Moore."

"Parker, please. Hello." Parker stood up and reached across the table to shake her hand.

"Hi, Sheila." Mitch shook her hand.

"How can we help you? Sorry for the rush, but it's getting a little crazy around here." Sheila kept looking over to the doorway. Her speech was pressured, body movements quick, and her eyes never stopped darting.

"We're here to discuss some union matters, and …" Mitch started only to have Sheila stop him.

"Excuse me." She got up as fast as she had sat down and took three quick steps out into the hallway.

"What the hell is this?" Parker leaned over to Mitch and whispered.

"Got no clue. It's been like this for weeks."

"Gentleman," Sheila darted back in without sitting down. She grabbed the notebook and papers she had come in with and began backing toward the door. "The governor needs me. I'm so sorry." She was gone.

The room was silent. Mitch and Parker sat motionless for a few moments as if painted on a canvas. No one moved.

"Please, follow me." The bodyguard, with his hands folded at his belt, was at the door.

Parker and Mitch stood and made their way out of the room.

"Well, now. That was productive," Parker quipped as they walked down the hall.

"Shuddup. Let's go get some coffee at the Silverbow and talk."

They exited the hallway followed by the guard. Once the two stepped toward the elevator, the guard stepped back into the hallway on the other side of the double-glass doors. Parker's thoughts turned toward the Silverbow and getting information from Mitch.

The elevator put them at street level. They walked out the front steps. The weather was typical Juneau. Some drizzle and fog. The coffeehouse was down Seward Street and right on 2nd.

"So, Mitch, without digging too much, what's going on up here with the oil and gas?"

"It's nuts. You have most in the state who want to drill every nook and cranny because it puts them to work. You've got the Republicans who want to drill to make gobs of money and claim there's enough to stop using so much foreign oil, and finally all of the environmental protection types that don't want anything touched because we should be developing alternative resources. How's that?"

They turned onto 2nd Street.

"That's a lot. Who's winning?"

"You know, Parker, I've got a lot of clients with a lot of land, and they're sitting on gold mines. Literally and figuratively."

"Gold gold or black gold?"

"Both. You know that." Mitch seemed perturbed. He knew Parker's intelligence. *What was this all about?*

"Yes. I do, and I'm sorry if I'm not articulating this correctly. Let's get some coffee and maybe I'll think better."

Parker opened the door to the quaint café and inn where he was the day before. He took a quick glance for the same two men but saw no one.

"Two black and one carrot cake." Parker's Silverbow favorite. "I got this one, Mitch." He paid the cashier and the two sat in the main part of the café.

"So, why the sudden interest?" Mitch started sipping his coffee.

"Curious. Seems like everything's at a standstill."

"It is. And you're paying about five bucks a gallon keeping it that way."

"Somebody's getting rich."

"A lot of people are, but more and more it's foreign interests. We don't own a lot of those companies anymore."

"The Native corporations are doing well." Parker hadn't touched his coffee. He was working on the carrot cake.

"Sure, when they can keep their boards straight. They go through people like water, but yes. They sit on a lot of assets."

"Interesting. So, where's the governor on all of this?"

"Who knows? She's become so mysterious, we're all wondering about a lot of stuff."

Parker was now drinking the coffee. He looked out the window and watched the fog begin to lift. The drizzle remained, but the sky was brightening.

"Interesting."

Now they both gazed outside.

★ ★ ★

It was early spring in 2008 when Parker finally had a chance to meet the governor without her staff. Since there were no campaign funds given to her by his company, Parker mostly received good wishes. There was always unsteadiness from her staff, as if something was going on but nobody should know. Politicians and their staffs in Juneau noticed a distancing from the governor. The more oil and gas prices went up, the less the governor was in view. Everything Mitch talked about was being confirmed.

Rumors surfaced about the presidential campaign. Parker found everything the NSA told him was also coming true. The good governor of the State of Alaska was on the road to bigger and better things—and like any other person who got in with the correct political crowd, she would never want for money for the rest of her life. People were getting rich through oil and gas and she would benefit. The spin in the media would be the public was getting what they wanted—a small-town mayor getting the best of the good old boys—but it was the good old boys playing bad guys all the way to the bank.

★ ★ ★

Parker made several trips to Juneau, although he continued to meet with Vic and Darryl in Anchorage. He never mentioned one to the other. He figured Vic knew everything. He also discovered more about his wife by combing the Internet and calling friends in Michigan. Just as Brooks and Ramsey had described, Stefanie was funneling money into investments outside of his control, and he received proof of her finding the wealthy investment banker.

It was a spring Saturday in 2008 when Parker decided to sleep in. He awoke at 10:00 a.m. It was 2:00 p.m. in Michigan. He walked to a bench on the Tony Knowles Trail that overlooked the Anchorage Port.

"Hi," he said into the phone.

"Where the fuck have you been?" She was driving. He could hear the wind and the traffic noise.

"I slept in." His shallow smile disappeared.

He remembered what Darryl told him: 'You'll never get the response you expect.'

"I was—just sleeping in." Parker was leaning down with his left hand covering his face while his right held the phone to his ear.

"Go back to fucking bed." She hung up.

Parker got off the bench and drove to the airport. Didn't pack a bag. Didn't take anything but his wallet. He flew back to Michigan to clean out his belongings from the house. The one he'd sunk thousands of dollars into. He left his furniture, paintings, flat-screen TVs, and all that he had bought for her and her children. He put his favorite blue-leather chair in storage. He decided it was time to change, as Darryl suggested. While Parker was at his house, he never saw her or talked to her. It was as if she knew everything he was doing or going to do.

He returned to Alaska two days later. Vic found him.

★ ★ ★

"So what's this about our Supreme Court?"

John Mansfield, Field Supervisor for the NSA, was being grilled by the Director of the Super PAC in the special room deep below NSA headquarters as he tried to get his notes up on his laptop. It was 3:00 a.m. in Fort Meade.

"We'll ma'am, a conversation from one of our CI's—" said Mansfield.

"Excuse me? A 'CI'?" interrupted a new member of the group.

"Sorry. That's a confidential informant," explained Mansfield. "We have many, but this one wears a wire to surveillance political arenas. The person has helped us in two states and D.C. and is now in a third state."

"A name? Is that okay?" the new member asked as he looked at the director sitting across from him.

"I'm sorry, sir. No," Mansfield replied and also turned his attention to the director.

"Mr. Miller," added the director as she looked at the newest member, "our sources are not revealed to anyone, for obvious reasons, unless absolutely necessary." She returned her stare at Mansfield. "Continue."

"We have a British gentleman, identity yet to be confirmed by voice patterns, who has been putting together a group of billionaires and wealthy officials of foreign governments to purchase political influence in the United States." Mansfield paused.

"This is *new?*" quipped another member of the Super PAC as he looked around the table, smiling.

"Mr. Morgan, it is new to the scale we're beginning to identify," chided the director.

"Anyway," Mansfield began again, "this group has infiltrated the highest levels of our government. We're also afraid that through the governor's staff in Illinois this group may have interceded in our CI's personal life. Nothing is confirmed yet."

The Super PAC members were silent. Except for the buzz of electronics in the room, there was no sound.

"We now wonder if this group knew about us obtaining our CI and began to manipulate him before we did." Mansfield closed his laptop.

"This CI …" Mr. Miller was about to ask a question, "Why can't we just stop using him?"

"We can't right now, but we will cut him loose as soon as possible. His life may be in danger and once cut loose, we may never see him again—alive."

Chapter 47

"**What the hell** is going on? We're getting great information from you and then you split to go home? Where is our wire and equipment?" Vic was not happy and had already contacted Brooks and Ramsey.

"I've about had it with everything, Vic. I cleaned out my house." The men were walking down 3rd Avenue by the Snow Goose Restaurant and Sleeping Lady Brewery. A beer sounded good.

"Alaskan Amber." Vic ordered a brew made famous by the Alaskan Brewing Company in Juneau.

"Pale, please," said Parker.

They walked up to the second level of the brewery so they could sit outside.

"Look, we have enough to put a connection between the oil, gas, and politicos but we need more details. There are more Chinese and Japanese lobbyists in Juneau than tourists. Brooks said the Super PAC is now interested in how the hospitals are funneling so much money for work on the Slope. Alaska's making a fortune on this stuff, but a lot of the money's going to other states and D.C." Vic looked out at the Cook Inlet.

Parker drank his beer and listened as he too gazed out over Cook Inlet.

"Parker, people have no clue how rich their elected officials are becoming. They just keep buying gas, bitching about the price at the pumps, and never look twice to see how much oil and gas stocks are rising and making the connection." Vic was shaking his head and staring into his beer. "The top's about to blow and your lady governor is going to be wealthy beyond belief once she's out of office." Vic paused. He looked around and leaned forward. "Ramsey has reliable information she's going to run as vice president. That's why she's hiding."

Parker listened. He was still thinking about cleaning out his house. He was no longer worried about the yelling, screaming, hitting, or the verbal abuse directed at his own children. But, what did he have left? Nothing. Constant worry about gathering information for the government and yet not knowing what day it was. He just kept listening.

"Parker? Wake the fuck up!"

"I'm here. Do you know every time I have lunch with those hospital goofs, drunken senators, and uneducated representatives I wanna puke? I win the grievances. I win the arguments, but what's in it for me? What? Nothing. I will end up with nothing. I've spent three fortunes on a woman I never want to see again. I've made enough political enemies to make Bush look like Mother Teresa, and have burned every bridge with every hospital and union across this country. I am so …"

Suddenly blood spattered on Parker's shirt. Vic fell to the floor. He'd been shot through the right upper chest. He was on the ground, struggling to get his weapon out. Parker was peering under the table when Vic grabbed him and threw him down next to him.

"Get the fuck down!" Vic yelled.

Chapter 48

No one else was on the deck. Parker lay next to Vic. He realized Vic had leaned over the table at that precise moment to get his attention. Vic and Parker pulled the metal table down in front of them.

"Parker, I'm okay, but you have to get outta here. I don't know where the shot came from, so we have to move this table with us to the door."

The door into the bar area was about ten feet away. The only place the shot could have come from was a building near Parker's apartment on 3rd Avenue. They pulled the table to the door and vaulted in. Vic was losing a lot of blood. Two people sitting at the bar just stared. The bartender, realizing what had happened, ran from behind the rows of taps and bottles to the two men on the floor.

"Call 911 and tell them officer down at the Snow Goose. Unknown location of shooter." Vic was very certain of his words. "Parker, you stay right by me."

The Anchorage Police Department was just two blocks away. The sirens were instantly heard after the phone call. Officers rushed upstairs, guns pointed at everyone. Others surrounded the area out front and around the bottom of the hill below. Vic pulled his ID and explained Parker was with him. The ambulance and fire personnel arrived and began to treat Vic. His wound was clean through. They started an IV and placed him on a stretcher. Vic explained what happened and told the commanding officer on the scene to take Parker to the station. He'd get a phone call soon explaining everything. Vic was taken to Providence Hospital while Parker was taken to the police station.

Chapter 49

"Mr. Moore? I'm Captain Edger. You want to tell me what happened?"

"We were having a beer. Next thing I know, Vic was down."

Parker was sitting at a table. A chair sat empty on the other side.

"Did you hear anything, see anything? Why were you there?" Edger was standing against the wall across from Parker.

"I can tell you I heard nothing. We were the only ones on the deck. That's what I know."

"Why were you there?" Edger came and sat down at the table.

"Sorry."

"Is there some reason you can't tell me?"

"Yes. You can ask that man right there."

Brooks was walking down the hallway toward them. Parker could see him through the window. Brooks came into the room. He was in jeans and a Washington Capitals sweatshirt.

"Wow. Don't know where you're from," Parker quipped.

"Shut up," was Brooks' harried reply. Brooks took a deep breath and looked at Edger. "Captain. John Brooks. Can we have a word outside?"

The captain nodded and the two men stepped into the hallway. Parker watched as he tried to put all the pieces together. Besides being on an adrenaline rush, he was numb from his recent mental state.

Brooks came into the room as Captain Edger walked down the hall. No expression on either man's face.

"You all right, Moore?"

"Yeah, thanks for asking. Vic?"

"He'll make it. We're moving you, though. You've got one more trip to D.C. to make for us, so we have to keep you alive. Come on."

Brooks and Parker left the police station and headed south down L Street and Minnesota Drive toward the airport. When Brooks pulled into the Millennium Hotel parking lot it was dark out. The hotel sat near Lake Spenard which was home to more seaplanes than people. Most lakes in the lower 48 had cottages and boats. This lake had planes to the same degree.

As soon as the car stopped, a man opened up Parker's door. Parker soon found himself being hustled out a back door of the hotel and into a seaplane by two men. Before he knew it, they were airborne and heading into the black.

Chapter 50

During the quick journey through the hotel and into the seaplane, not a word was spoken. The men treated Parker politely, but with the concentration of a Navy SEAL team on a mission. Finally, after about fifteen minutes in the air, one of the men spoke.

"Mr. Moore, we work with Vic. Agent Brooks notified us immediately and asked us to take you to a safe house. We can't tell you where you're going, but you'll be safe. How are you feeling?"

"Honestly? I need to pee and I'm starving. Other than that, I don't have a clue."

The man sitting behind Parker handed him a urinal. "The best we can do is offer you water and the urinal. Food will have to wait."

Parker took the urinal and stared at it. There wasn't any privacy, but it didn't really matter. He looked out the window pretending he was on a boat and could pee over the side. Then he got to business using the urinal.

As the trip progressed, Parker's adrenaline edge subsided and the drone of the engine put him to sleep. He had no idea how long they were in the air. The man sitting behind Parker pushed back and forth on his shoulder.

"Mr. Moore? Mr. Moore? We're about to land."

The plane circled a couple times and there were lights along the shore. Suddenly some lights under the water were illuminated. The plane touched down like it was daylight. All Parker could think was that these guys weren't your average cops. They pulled around after landing, and Parker saw a man waiting on a dock holding a rope. They tied up and the door opened.

"Hello, Mr. Moore. My name is Matthews. I'll be your host."

As soon as Parker was on the dock, the plane was untied. As he walked up a grassy slope, he heard the loud roar of the motor. The plane was gone. All the lights were extinguished except for a few in the cabin ahead of him.

There was the scent of the ever-present willow in the air. A cool night at the end of August was refreshing. Parker figured they were somewhere near Lake Clark on the west side of Cook Inlet, but really had no clue. He just had a suspicion they'd take him to a part of the state where there were no roads, which was most of Alaska.

The cabin was well furnished. Much like the lodges he'd read about or heard others describe: fireplace, snowshoes hanging on the wall, open kitchen with a professional gas stove that could cook for a small army, and all the fishing and hunting accoutrements one would expect.

"Mr. Moore—" Matthews started.

Parker cut him off. "Parker. The name's Parker."

"Fine. Parker, make yourself at home. You're an important person and we're going to take good care of you."

Parker noticed the Glock on Matthews' hip. He also noticed the room to the left of the kitchen that was bathed in an eerie green light and was full of computer screens, radios, and other electronics.

Parker walked over to the extra-large side-by-side fridge and looked inside. He grabbed the Ben and Jerry's Mud Pie and walked over to the leather chair facing the fireplace. A small fire remained. Matthews sat in the twin leather chair to Parker's right. As Matthews sat with his elbows on his knees leaning forward toward the fire, Parker took a deep breath and sat back, slouching as far down as his big frame would allow.

"What the hell happened? I'm having a beer. I'm in the police station. I'm on a plane. I'm here." Parker just stared at the flame.

"Well," Matthews said, as he sat back in the chair to look

directly at Parker, "I can tell you that you're pretty deep in the bush and safe. I can also tell you it may be a few days before you go anywhere. Until then, just stay close. If you go out, there's an extra sidearm in the cabinet. Brooks told me you have history and know how to handle a weapon. There's a .357 holstered and ready. Bears by the way, not people."

Parker ate the ice cream. He always wondered about places like this. When he was a baby living in Mountain View, Alaska, his father was a communications specialist stationed at Fort Richardson. Oftentimes his mother would be notified that her husband wasn't coming home, and nobody could tell her when he'd be back. During the Cold War in the late 1950s, there was constant work on secret landing strips, missile sites, and radar equipment. While the U2 planes flew over the Soviet Union, there would always be air-rescue planes at several of those sites around Alaska just sitting with their engines running. The air crews never knew why. Keep the engines running was all they were told.

Communication lines and right-of-ways were sliced and diced all over the Frontier State. Parker's father told him many people lost their lives in the bush during those years. The Cold War had victims but no heroes. While his father was lucky to have had a tent, Parker was in the lap of luxury. The government and military sure were different now.

Chapter 51

Parker slept like he hadn't in years. He did it without scotch and without a pill. In the aftermath of the shooting, the plane ride, and a late night talking with Matthews, he'd forgotten about his life. The rush of the adventure had caught up with him. No abuse. No screaming. No union subversion. No politicians looking for money. But—what about his position? How will Brooks explain Parker missing? What about the press?

He sat on the porch with a cup of coffee, thinking so fast he just stood up and began to walk. A trail to the left was cleared of alders and scrub along the water. He walked with his head up. If a brownie was near, Parker had plenty of open space to see.

He suddenly stopped and turned toward the lake. Who the hell would shoot at him? Maybe it was Vic. It's not like a thousand people from the Slope wouldn't want him dead if they found out he was the deep cover on the drug bust. Parker had been so caught up in his personal life, he'd lost track of everything. Had he been found out? The wire was so sophisticated and he'd been doing it for so long … he wandered. Every so often he'd stop to look around and take a deep breath.

"Moore? Moore?!" Matthews was yelling.

Parker completely forgot to tell him he was taking a walk. He jumped into a clearing.

"Here! I'm here."

Matthews walked off the porch and made his way to Parker. The lake was gray reflecting a gray sky. There was a range to the west, but clouds covered most everything. A cool mist made its way across the lake.

"Don't do that, Moore. I gotta know where you are, and you forgot the sidearm." Matthews seemed genuinely concerned.

"Sorry. I couldn't stop thinking about everything. How are they going to explain my absence and what happened at the Snow Goose?"

"That's why I was looking for you. It's Saturday, so we have some time about the work thing. Nobody's looking for you. The press goes by the police blotter and Brooks had the captain release the shooting details about an unidentified man sitting by himself enjoying a beer. Vic's fine. After a debriefing, he definitely took one for you. Sounds like he leaned over toward you and got a through-n-through near the shoulder. Someone was going for you; we have to find out why. Let's get back to the house, have some breakfast, and go over the past couple months."

"I could use some bacon and eggs. You got that?"

"We have whatever you want. Let's have a day, Parker. A little breakfast, some talk, and we'll hit the water. You fish?"

Parker was an avid fisherman. He tied his own flies and hit the water every chance he had. Except for this year, he and his sons were on a ten-year run for an annual fishing trip. Suddenly he felt a wave of his old self. A lifting of the constant pressure.

"You bet."

They headed for the cabin.

Chapter 52

Parker's attorney was trying to locate Parker to inform him there were five men at the house in Okemos when he delivered the divorce papers to Stefanie. There was a guy mowing the lawn, a couple guys working in the house, and one doing something in the pole barn. The attorney was also going to tell Parker his soon-to-be-former wife was dressed in a black pencil skirt, four-inch stilettos, and a revealing white blouse when she came to the door. She accepted the papers with a smile.

Parker's therapist was trying to find him to reschedule Monday's appointment. Their last session covered the angry physical attacks she perpetrated and the time she almost ran him over in the driveway. Parker was trying to regain his dignity and self-respect, but at the same time, he had become more depressed. Being in charge of the largest health-care union in Alaska was the easy part. The shooting at the Snow Goose was just a week after Parker confided to Darryl that he was suicidal. Parker recalled the conversation.

"I'm going to clean out the house and file for divorce."

"You ready for everything that goes with it?" asked Darryl.

"I have no idea. I just know that after my daughter left, I can't live this life. I thought about ending it all. I mean, not like I have a plan, but doing something reckless." Parker did not tell him about staring into a gun case.

"You need to give yourself time to heal. It could take a while."

"Time is something I don't have. In fact, I want out of everything. I kept two cars, a blue chair, and some sporting goods. After years as an executive, educator, lobbyist, and business owner, that's all I have."

"You have family, successful children, and years ahead of you."

"I don't want anything. I want to hide for the rest of my life."

"Okay. And do what?" Darryl wasn't letting Parker off the hook.

"You mean if I don't kill myself?"

"Yes. You'd be alive."

"Write. I want to write. I want to fish and spend time with the kids. Oh, and paint. Should I be on meds?" Parker felt tangential.

"Parker, you're exhausted. You haven't stopped for almost twenty years. You've been in an abusive marriage with a borderline wife, and you're depressed. We've talked about meds. We decided no. How's the drinking?"

"The tours of Scotland by bottle seem to keep me busy. Less airline miles," Parker said with a half-smile.

In five minutes, Parker went from regaining his identity through depression and being self-destructive to humor. He'd become as bad a personality disorder as he'd been living with. Parker still hadn't been honest with Darryl, and he knew nothing of Parker's undercover work or his reactionary spending. Parker often wondered if he'd be different if he'd just cold-cocked Stefanie—how different his life might be.

"Darryl?"

"Yeah Parker?"

"I think I've become the borderline."

★ ★ ★

Parker finished breakfast and was cleaning up the dishes. He put the last plate down and stared out the window, dish towel over his shoulder and both hands resting on the sink. Clouds and mist were lifting. The black spruce couldn't hide the head of the bull moose chewing on a willow branch in the thicket at the edge of the forest. Matthews had fly rods in hand and waders on the porch.

"Parker? Come on, let's fish."

Parker put his head down and threw the towel in the sink. He turned and tried to think about Rainbow and Dolly Varden.

After some time on the water, Matthews started with the questions. "So, Moore, did you notice anything out of the ordinary the last few weeks?"

"You mean, like walking around in a haze; gathering information on politicians, lobby groups, and union groups; wearing a wire; and living in fear of my life from all of them and my abusive wife? No, nothing different."

"Come on. Work with me here. Any different people? Events?" Matthews continued to cast.

"Actually, no. After I cleaned out my house in Michigan, I flew back and met Vic."

"What about in Juneau?"

"No. Well, I noticed new security around the governor's office. One guy kept staring at me and was talking on his cell while he watched me. She's got a shit load of people around her all of a sudden."

"Anything in Anchorage, Fairbanks, or Ketchikan?"

"No."

Matthews never stopped throwing his Adams onto the quiet lake surface. Parker was lost in his rhythm. Ten and two. Ten and two. Parker loved the rhythm of the outdoors. He often thought of one of the final lines in *The Hunt for Red October* when Sean Connery said he missed the peace of fishing. Parker missed everything peaceful. Neither he nor Matthews caught anything, but the time on the water was good medicine.

They walked back to the cabin. Matthews put away the gear while Parker went to the liqueur cabinet. A good fishing lodge was sure to have some single malt. He found Glenlivit, Glenfiddich, and even Talisker, but once he spotted the Lagavulin, he grabbed it and poured four fingers worth in a crystal glass. The warmth along with the strong odor of peat and seaweed brought a deep breath to Parker as he closed his eyes for a second sip. He walked over to the leather chair by the fireplace while Matthews entered the communications room.

Parker sat down and thought of the smallmouth bass and northern pike he and the kids would catch in the U.P. He saw himself on the front of the bass boat casting toward the flats near Deer Park Lodge where George would always try to catch the big one so Mike and Monica would show everyone at the lodge store. Parker would fish till he and the boys decided to dock and walk to the store for their daily ice cream. His daydreaming was interrupted by Matthews walking in front of him. Matthews stopped and looked down.

"Do you know a guy called Ice Pick?"

"Yeah. He was my union exec in Chicago. The board had me fire him after he almost blew the University of Chicago contract. I felt bad. He was actually a pretty good guy."

Matthews moved to the other leather chair and sat facing Parker.

"Turns out he showed up in Anchorage. They traced trajectories and found an apartment in your building with his stuff in it. They waited till he came back and grabbed him. The rifle and scope were in a closet. After some questioning, he came clean."

"Pete. I'll be damned. Does he know I didn't want to fire him?"

"Guess not. Doesn't matter. What's important is that it's Sunday and you have to be at the office tomorrow like nothing happened. Your cover's not blown. You just have some enemies out there."

Parker sat back and mumbled, "Just the same old shit."

"Brooks said you have a visit with Stimson next week." Matthews looked into the fire.

"Senator Stimson. Ranking member of the Republican Party and a fine resident of Girdwood."

"Yup. And suddenly in a new house." Matthews played along.

"Wow, you mean maybe he's getting money from someone or doing favors for people? You jest." Parker took another sip.

Matthews shook his head and laughed as he stood up.

"Plane will be here in a couple hours. Be ready."

Parker sat and watched the fire as he sipped the scotch. He had to return to reality and face the world.

Chapter 53

On Monday, Parker left his apartment on 3rd Avenue and drove to the office on Northern Lights. He unlocked the door and felt the same despair he'd felt before he went back to Michigan to remove his belongings from the house.

He stared out the large window on the north wall of his office at the Chugach. The bright morning sun altered the face of the mountains as they traversed south. Parker sat for a good hour with his feet on the desk. He looked at the awards, plaques, diplomas, and memorabilia one by one, stopping at a union award he was given in Chicago; he then looked back to the mountains. Beyond the valley and out toward Palmer was the same suburban sprawl you'd find in Colorado. Eagle River could be Boulder or Estes Park. The only difference from Jackson Hole, Wyoming, was the cut of the mountains. The same fast food, the same coffee shops, and recently even the same people inhabited the area.

Parker began to tick off the things that had happened since Brooks and Ramsey walked up his porch. The governor of Illinois would be indicted. Everyone would bump heads trying to get out of the way, but most of the political cronies and lobbyists were part of the story. They were culpable but would hide. In Michigan, there was work afoot to check the stories of senators and representatives doing the same type of strong-arming for political funding. In Alaska, the knowledge gained about the wealth behind a yet unknown public move by the governor would make for amazing press. The public still didn't realize a new party on the horizon would make the largest attempt since President Hoover to guarantee new millionaires on every block regardless of the cost to most people. The NSA knew the good governor of Alaska would not be in Juneau to finish. Michigan, Illinois, and Alaska—three states and lots of political fallout. Nobody that anyone talked with or questioned even thought about what Parker had provided in all these cases. He still couldn't believe an investigative journalist had not contacted him. The fear in the shooting was that someone had. Poor Pete. A good Teamster to the last.

The Alaska story wasn't closed yet, but a trip to D.C. and a meeting with Senator Stimson would most likely sound the senator's death knell. Now the unions would be getting their comeuppance. Especially in Alaska, the plight of the union struggle was obvious. Many of the union leaders were conservative Republicans. They had no knowledge of the history of the labor movement, socialist beliefs, or even how the Manifesto played a role. When Parker talked about the history and how it could work in organizing and retaining union members, several of the board members tuned out. Their interests were not only wages and benefits, but getting the supervisor in trouble or fired. Parker was placed in the role of bad guy over and over again to win grievances and arbitrations for trivial arguments and mostly for employees he would never hire. The national movements connected to his union group were all about the revenue. Membership counts and political clout were paramount. Power and money that the unions argued against for the good capitalists and the health-care systems were exactly what the unions had as their top agenda item. They wanted power to gain enough clout to press the membership which brought in more revenue to build bigger and better union bureaucracy along with union executive salaries. The unions were nothing but free market machines where the widgets were people. The lines were blurred beyond belief. Parker was working with borderline personalities and borderline businesses.

NSA interest was piqued by the volumes of cash coming into the union PACs from sources no one documented. A push for national health care wasn't about what may be good for overall health and wellness, but how union members could be counted like dollar bills rolling out of the Denver Mint. Factories and general manufacturing, once the bastion of unions, were gone. Only so many service workers and state and federal workers could be unionized, and if they were, the wages didn't produce great amounts of dues revenue. Health care was another matter. Physicians were unionizing. Nurses were joining and pharmacists were discussing unions. National health care might make sense from an efficiency and human decency perspective, but it was also rich loam for growing unions.

Parker was startled from his thoughts by the ring of the phone.

"Parker, can you book me a flight for our Washington trip? First class, please. I think I deserve it." The union president, Diane, didn't think twice about spending money. In fact, Parker had discovered that the previous executive ran a private business from the union office, and the last office manager was using thousands of air miles on Alaska Air that were technically union property.

The phone rang again.

"Parker? This is Darryl. I left messages for you and wanted to make sure you knew I changed our appointment for today."

Parker's feet came off the desk and he suddenly became interested in the present. He put his elbows on the desk and ran his right hand through his hair.

"Darryl, I have so much to tell, um, talk about. I'm sorry. I haven't even looked at the cell phone."

"Tomorrow at 9:00 a.m. Is that okay?"

"Yes. I'll be there."

Parker wanted to see Darryl now. He'd forgotten about the appointment, but wanted to unload. He lied about checking his cell phone. He'd looked to see if she'd called or left a message about every two minutes since his return on Sunday evening. Then, like a borderline would expect of the partner, Parker longed for a conversation, an indication that he existed. Giving that kind of power to a borderline was devastating on a person's capacity to think, work, and even breathe. The abuse may have ended, but the mental scarring was thick.

At Darryl's urging, Parker had picked up his old textbooks again. He also read *Stop Walking on Eggshells* and bought the workbook. Parker was learning that while he wasn't the borderline, he was maintaining the relationship and putting all he knew at risk. He was as sick as she was—actually worse. Her personality disorder didn't qualify as a mental illness whereas his reactionary depression, suicidal thoughts, and combined dissociative state did.

No one came into the office that day and the only thing Parker accomplished was ordering the first-class airline ticket for the union president. An unhappy union president was a bad thing. Parker was getting close to not really giving a shit.

When he left his office and began to drive, he was tempted to leave the state. Then he changed his mind. He thought about going to Seward to hang out by the water. Maybe Denali. He loved Teklanika. The problem was the distances. Nothing in Alaska was close. He settled for the Tony Knowles Trail. His favorite bike ride was up past Earthquake Park. He loved smelling the salt air and stopping along the way. He'd often sit at the lagoon and write.

Chapter 54

Parker rode the elevator up to the fifth floor of the Denali Building in Anchorage and sat in the waiting room. Darryl had the typical office setup with a waiting room separate from the therapy room exit. That way confidentiality was maintained while comfort was instilled in the private waiting area.

"Parker? Come in. How are you?" Darryl stuck out his hand to shake. Parker hugged him and held on. "Whoa. All right, all right. I get it. Let's sit and get to work."

Parker started, "I need to tell you something. I was visiting with a friend at Snow Goose the other day, and someone took a shot at me. Turns out it was my old labor exec from Chicago. He ended up in my apartment building and set up shop with a rifle and scope. Do you fucking believe that? I know she put him up to it." Parker was showing real emotion. The automaton was gone. "I always suspected they were together when she visited me in Chicago and disappeared downtown. He was always on the road, so I never really knew where he was—not that I asked. I suspected it when the board members threatened my job and career if I didn't get rid of him. I really liked the guy. I know he mucked up the University of Chicago, but I fixed it. He was just trying to figure out the union business outside of the Teamsters, but anyway, she screamed at me when I gave him his severance and walking papers. It was one of those all-night deals where I ended up locked in the kid's room with her screaming. I should have just … no. I would never hit back. You don't hit women."

"I read about the shooting. You weren't mentioned, Parker. What's going on?" Darryl leaned forward in his chair. Parker always sat on the soft loveseat. Darryl sat in a hardback side chair off to Parker's right. The windows behind showed the same Chugach that Parker looked at from his office.

"Darryl, I can't tell you," Parker stammered. He was trying not to think faster than his mouth would go, but suddenly everything hit him. He stared at Darryl; his eyes welled up. "I don't know what the press said. They were told to keep me out."

"Okay. I don't believe you, but if that's where we're at right now, that's where we're at. How's the scotch?"

"Speyside. I toured Islay after the shooting but slept like a baby without drinking to sleep." Parker was looking out the window and wiping his eyes. "I figured the Highlands weren't strong enough. Darryl, I need to get out. I mean, out of everything, and I don't care what happens to me."

"Are you thinking of harming yourself?"

"No. Really, I'm not. Last time? Yes. Now? No. I want to go back to my kids … the fishing trips … and get the hell out of this life."

Parker turned his gaze toward Darryl as he leaned forward. Darryl was sitting back in his chair with a foot on the coffee table; his right hand rubbed his bearded chin while he listened.

"I'm so torn between making the pitch for the average Joe while at the same time making the system work for everyone who has or wants the money … and there is so much money floating around. The worst part? They're all just like my abusive wife. It's so cutthroat, and if you make one mistake, you're gone. They get rid of you like trash on the corner. I feel like I'm in the can and people are grabbing the handles."

The two sat in silence for some moments. Darryl got up, walked over to his desk, and picked up the newspaper. He brought it back and laid it in front of Parker.

"You going to tell me what's going on?"

"Darryl, I can't. I can't. I'm sure it will all come out in the wash. I will tell you this ..." Parker stopped.

He didn't know if he should say anything. He'd lost track of reality and boundaries, and yet, that's exactly why he started to meet with Darryl. Living in a borderline world was debilitating, especially when there was no respite. Both his career and personal life were diagnosable.

"I've been working undercover for the feds. They approached me before I moved here. All that stuff in Illinois with the governor? I was wearing a wire. I wasn't the only one they were working with, but I got enough. Without the abuse in my life, this could be a blast, maybe even exciting, but I have no rest until I hit the scotch and go to bed at night. Even then, it's not sleep. It's extended nightmares. And now, I'm getting shot at. I have absolutely no idea what I've done by the end of a week."

Parker had lost all strength and inner resolve. This large man had nothing left. He wasn't a badge-carrying man on the job. He wasn't a fully invested lobbyist or executive since he was only doing it for some loose reason connected to threats. He was a man in between worlds. He wasn't in control of anything—and until he met Stefanie he had always been in control of everything. He didn't have a home or family. Everything he had at one point in his life was gone.

Darryl studied Parker in silence. After several minutes he said, "Thank you. You're going to be okay."

★　★　★

Stefanie would get in her car and drive down Grand River to the Speedway gas station by the Meridian Mall. The coffee was always fresh and the guys in the store loved watching her sashay in. She knew it too, so the guys always made sure they had her favorite hazelnut-flavored creamer in stock. On her way to work, she listened to the Dave Matthews Band. Never a worry because she had everyone around her to do the worrying for her. In a beautiful borderline dance, everyone waltzed around her needs and wants. A simple job, a lot of money, and everyone to watch her was just about enough for life. At work, she'd sometimes have flashbacks of Parker showing up with flowers or sending her romantic poetry. She'd smile, shake her head, and start to open the mail. That was about the toughest part of her day.

Blair, her latest victim, was happy he had found a woman to be his third wife as he'd let his wives go once they reached an age when they no longer lived up to his standards. *This one*, he thought, *would last for a long time. She was sleek and sassy.* Her experiences met the needs of an investment banker, and her looks brought him more customers. *A match made in heaven.*

Chapter 55

After a couple quiet days, Parker found himself on the flight to D.C. Senator Stimson was starting to feel some heat from the press leaks Brooks put out about construction done on his Girdwood residence. NSA knew the money had come from the hospital lobby, but to Stimson's credit, he wasn't the only one in Washington to funnel money for personal use. He was simply the one everyone was ready to get rid of. A new regime was coming in, the leader being from his home state, and it was his turn to be taken out to the curb. Parker was arriving with the wire and three union officials to put the lid on the trash can.

Unknown to Brooks, Ramsey, Vic, Darryl, or anyone else, Parker had begun to plan his escape. He called an old attorney friend who he sent referrals to on a regular basis for some pro bono advice. Parker knew the board members who wanted him as the bad guy would be furious if he left. Their scheme of protection would be gone. He also knew his divorce was final in a week, and he'd go home to nothing. There was always his mom's hideaway on the river in Northern Michigan. He could feel the river run by him as he fly-fished for brook trout. The kids driving up and everyone laughing around the campfire. No work and no stress was only a decision away. He couldn't hit his wife, but the courage to do something different was returning. He wanted his life back. His attorney friend said it could take a few years or more to sort out, but that was the risk he'd take.

As the plane's landing gear came down and they approached Reagan International Airport, he could feel the anger swell and his game face come on. They were all a bunch of mother fuckers who needed to be brought down. If he couldn't touch her as she drove around Ingham County singing out the window of her car, the other bastards would take the fall. Hate just created more hate, and he had enough to fill the entire Jordon River on a good baptismal day. He really was acting as a misanthropic borderline.

The plane landed and taxied toward the gate. The flight attendants were making the last announcements of weather reports and flight connections. Parker, with his eyes closed, began to wonder how he would leave Alaska and make border crossings into the Yukon and Montana without anyone knowing. The plane came to a halt. Parker opened his eyes. He was ready.

Chapter 56

Parker grabbed his bags at the first carousal and walked outside into the taxi line. A taxi pulled up for him. Ramsey was driving.

"Is this a promotion?" Parker asked.

"Yes. I get great tips for the information I can give people. You should see what I got from the FOX reporter." Ramsey looked at Parker through the rearview mirror.

Parker had developed a nice relationship with Brooks and Ramsey. Even though they knew of his wife's affairs, violence, and use of his money, they didn't know how deep his depression was.

"This is a tricky one, Parker. Stimson is smart and has used his knowledge and political savvy to get whatever he needed or wanted. Don't be surprised if he hedges at every turn." Ramsey was making his way through heavy traffic as he talked.

"I'm thinking this will be hard because the three people I'm doing this with love Stimson. They're probably already ahead of us." Parker was getting anxious to finish this.

"One more thing, the Super PAC members running this operation through NSA have opened the door to a couple of people we don't know about. They didn't trust us any more than we trusted them. Stimson is suspected of being one of those in the know."

"Great. Do I get assassinated when this is done?" Parker was being sarcastic but had wondered just how they were going to let him go.

"Stimson faces a myriad of charges and complaints. He's done. No one is going to assassinate you except maybe me if you don't stop acting squirrelly. Don't forget, Parker, as the NSA, we know everything. And I mean everything. We listen to all." Ramsey was smiling but serious. He couldn't afford to have Parker Moore off on a tangent as this investigation wound down.

"This guy has had so many favors from his constituents over the years, we can't count them all. I'd be surprised if he paid for a cup of coffee at the 7-Eleven. But, we like the guy because he's done so much for our part of the government. Still doesn't make it right, though."

"So, this is a case where anything goes until somebody wants you gone? Then suddenly people start pointing fingers?" Parker was looking at the Washington Monument.

"Come on, Parker, you know that's how it is. You know that could be your fate."

Ramsey stopped along the Potomac Parkway to fit the wire on Parker. He had instructions to facilitate the meeting as he normally would. With Parker's help, all hell was about to break loose. Stimson was the last piece of the puzzle. If they could get Stimson to openly discuss his backing of the hospitals against Parker's legislation, they could equate that to the amount of money he just received from them connected to the five lobby visits from the hospital association along with some of the new work done on his house in Girdwood.

The NSA was also about to leak a study citing members of the House and Senate doing well in the stock market from insider trading tips they received as they awarded contracts through committees. That was much more acceptable in their minds than actual insider tips. Nonetheless, it had been going on for years. Some legislators would be investigated for the insider trading. Parker would be done, and he knew exactly what he was going to do once he was back in Anchorage.

Chapter 57

Ramsey dropped off Parker at the Hay-Adams Hotel. This was one of Parker's favorite places to stay. It was an historic boutique hotel on Lafayette Square directly across from the White House. As Parker waited to check in, he recalled a visit this past summer. He closed his eyes and began to feel the anger.

He had just finished a toast at a reception of union leaders and legislators gathered as a memorial to a fellow union executive who had died the month before. He exited the reception area and was feeling the sadness of losing a colleague who'd helped him through some tough professional decisions. As he entered his hotel room the phone rang.

"Hello?"

"What the hell are you doing? Do you know what fucking time it is?" She was furious.

"Honey, I have no idea. You know I was giving the final toast tonight. Why are you so upset?" Parker found himself angry. He glanced at the clock; it was only 9:00 p.m.

"I don't care who died. I care you haven't called me for two hours."

"Okay. Okay. I'm sorry. I should have taken the phone with me and called as soon as I was done, but …" Parker was stoic and robotic. It was a replay of the same call he'd had day in and day out for two years.

"Why don't you just stay there and die?" The line went dead.

Parker sat on the bed, simply holding the receiver, waiting for a dial tone. He looked at his reflection in the window against the blackness of the night. He hung up the phone and lay on the bed, still wearing his suit and tie. He woke up two hours later, only to throw his clothes on the floor and crawl underneath the bedspread.

"Mr. Moore?"

Parker opened his eyes slowly to the sound of the front desk attendant. He looked around to make sure he was still standing in the lobby of the hotel. Now he was becoming dissociative, and as he came back to the present, he felt his fists clench—almost as hard as his teeth were.

"Mr. Moore? Your room number and key. Please let us know if you need anything." The clerk saw the blankness in Parker's stare.

Parker made his way to the elevator and his room. He finished putting away his clothes and walked back downstairs and outside. The Stimson meeting was not until 4:00 p.m., after session was over, so Parker had changed into some shorts. He headed for his favorite bench in Lafayette Square. He sat and watched the tourists walk by the White House now cordoned off on both ends of Pennsylvania Avenue for safety purposes. The Capitol Police had cars posted 24/7 on each end and an officer walking in front. One could only guess the number of cameras and undercover personnel in the area. And there was always an anti-war, anti-nuclear, anti-everything person or people sitting out front stating their case.

Parker had his journal and wrote. He'd given most everything away in the divorce. The furniture, house, pictures, appliances, lawn tractors, everything was connected to violence, hate, and deceit. He wanted nothing connected to the past. He also prepared for his meeting with Senator Stimson. The meetings were routine, especially with Republicans, and the mental preparation was short. Any social legislation or any legislation having to do with union wishes was essentially ignored. The legislator was always briefed by lobbyists from the other side that usually included bigger dinners and more drinks than Parker could offer. In this case, the senator would act as if he was well versed on the subject.

Chapter 58

The entrance for guests and lobbyists was at the rear of the Capitol building. All credentials and packages were inspected before you were allowed inside. Once past the cacophony of visitors in the gathering space for tours, you went down the hallway to the front, ending up at the registration area to obtain a pass.

Parker had passes for the three union executives who all happened to be women and strong Republicans. They were backers of Stimson even though every vote he made was against organized labor. In Alaska, Stimson was the resurrection. Building projects, military spending, oil resources, you name it, Stimson got it for Alaska. He knew how to do it better than anyone. Alaska was the richest state, yet it received billions in federal dollars. The Last Frontier still had bush communities you could equate with the rain forests in the Amazon except for temperatures at the other end of the thermometer. By most accounts, the people who lived in those communities did so by choice. The Native corporations were very large and very rich. They controlled huge tracts of land and all the resources that went with them. Senator Stimson helped Alaska maintain a détente with the outside world to let it all grow.

Parker had one focus: to get the hospitals to stop working health-care staff extra hours over already long shifts where errors would become a dime a dozen and patients were at risk. Hospitals didn't want to hire more people to add to their payroll costs, they wanted to keep growing profit margins. The lawsuit potentials were enormous, but that's what good insurance and good attorneys were for. They were cheaper than hiring more people to take care of the sick. After all, the industrial revolution had reached health care and it was now the driving force in employment for most communities in the country. The dirty little secret of people dying due to errors only reared its ugly head every so often, and Americans had such short attention spans.

Besides Native Healthcare, there was only one other hospital system in Anchorage—and all of Alaska for that matter—Providence. Parker knew Providence had Stimson in its back pocket, but the effort for both sides of an argument was worth the work. The amount of people Providence employed made them an important player in the state. They were attempting to gobble up as much competition as possible with purchases and mergers. It didn't matter as long as they gained control. Stimson was their main focus for access to the Slope, and the wealth in health-care revenues available to the biggest player. Native influence may have a say in the development of the land, but the worker-bees were mostly out of the jurisdiction of the Native Healthcare system.

Parker walked his constituents down the hall, accompanied by the senator's Chief of Staff. They were in front of the Senate Majority Leader's office on Capitol Hill; one of the most powerful places in the world. A staff person opened the door.

"Mr. Moore?" The senator was standing and ready. He looked much shorter and older in person than he did on TV.

"Senator, thank you for your time today." Parker was careful of his imposing size.

"Ladies, please, let me give you a tour first." The senator shook their hands and held the door. Senator Stimson showed them the view from his office and adjoining balconies, which was where the Presidential inaugurations took place on the Capitol steps.

The senator's long-time assistant followed the group and watched everyone carefully. Parker was suddenly aware of his wire. The assistant wouldn't take her eyes off Parker, and he began to have suspicions that she knew. The clipboard she held close to her chest gave her an element of mystery, as if they were being interviewed and followed by an old grade-school teacher. Every so often she would write something while staring at Parker.

After the tour, they settled into classic soft-leather chairs like you would find around a lodge fireplace. The senator sat in a wooden chair higher than everyone else to allow his small stature a commanding pose over the discussion. At this level of politics, no detail was left out in the power plays, including how you were seated in a room.

As was often the case, the senator sat quietly, waiting for someone to begin the conversation and actual reason for the visit.

"Senator, we appreciate the audience today." Parker smiled even though he knew it sounded as if he were talking to the Pope. He also knew that's exactly how Stimson liked it.

"Audience? Please. I have no ring to kiss. How can I help?" It was as if Stimson could read Parker's mind.

"Well, while we're here lobbying, or should I say suggesting, some federal legislation, we thought we could ask for your help at the state level. We have a hospital system that covers the entire northwest section of the United States, with facilities in Alaska as well."

"Providence. Yes, I heard you've already organized one of the hospitals on the Kenai and are looking to organize the other two. Rather ambitious for a newcomer, don't you think?" Stimson was sitting forward, smiling and gazing at the women.

"Yes, well, that is the business I'm in, and the people before you have asked me to do that," Parker found himself off guard, but in this business, he quickly adapted. "Actually, Senator, those organizing campaigns are a direct result of why we're here. Those facilities have people working twelve-hour shifts and then asking them to stay four, six, or even another twelve hours extra without rest or consideration for their families."

"Don't physicians have to work that long?"

"In teaching hospitals, interns and residents do have those types of hours, but they are allowed sleep breaks, special lounges, and those hours are being challenged around the country on account of increasing errors in medications, treatment, and care. Senator, hospital systems prefer not to hire the necessary staff knowing laws about abandoning patients create a gray area for health-care professionals. They can keep their profit margins as high as they want, but organizing efforts will continue."

"We can't work those hours anymore," said Diane. "We're too old."

"So am I, Miss. So am I. I think you all know we can't get the kind of numbers to work in certain areas of Alaska as other places in the country. Now that you have these new contracts, Mr. Moore, perhaps you should just work out those issues during your negotiations instead of trying to pass a law forcing everyone to follow a new regulation. A new rule we probably don't need."

"You know, that's a good point," chimed in another union member.

Parker was worried that three Republican union members and Stimson supporters would essentially make this visit worthless. He was becoming convinced that Stimson knew about the wire, and wasn't going to say anything to add to the already building turmoil around his Girdwood residence.

"There, you see, Mr. Moore, even your folks think that's the way you should go."

Parker was careful not to change his affect or the way he was sitting. He even tried to control the size of his pupils so as to not give away his frustration, anger, and growing cynicism.

"So, you've spoken to the several Providence lobbyists?" Parker was baiting, but he really didn't care at that moment. He had decided how he was getting out of this.

"Well, now. That's a question normally not asked, Mr. Moore. But, I will answer it. Yes. Just like I'm talking with you. They have a right to their side of the story, wouldn't you agree?"

Stimson was now sitting back in his chair with his hands folded, looking smug. His head was cocked to the right and he was smiling at Parker. The women stared at Parker, waiting for his next move. Diane, the head of the constituency and the biggest

Stimson supporter had an angry scowl on her face. This was the same woman who came into the union office demanding Parker get her supervisor fired, along with all the other supervisors, because she thought the hospital was lower than the devil himself.

"Fair enough, Senator Stimson. We'll see what happens in the end. I respect your position, but I have thousands asking me to carry this message; so consider it delivered."

"Thank you, Mr. Moore. Now, will you ladies excuse us for a moment? I have a private matter to discuss with Mr. Moore."

The women exited the room as Stimson stood up and shook their hands. He whispered something to his assistant. The clipboard-toting woman escorted the others into another part of the senator's office. He heard her ask them for drink orders on the way out.

Parker wasn't sure what to expect. After similar spanks in Michigan and Illinois, he wasn't afraid, but he wasn't sure what this one was about.

Chapter 59

"Parker, is it? Do you mind?"

Parker smiled and stood. "That's fine, Senator."

Stimson shut the door.

"Sit. Sit." Parker sat down in the leather chair. "My colleagues from Michigan and Illinois told me you were rather forceful in your approach. I respect that. At least we know where you're coming from, and we know you don't have other clients to protect by treating us cautiously like some of your fellow slime-bag lobbyists. Please keep that off the record."

Parker smiled and nodded. Conscious of his wire, he actually took the comment as a compliment.

"However, I do want to say that you should keep your nose clean on this one. There are a lot of people lining up in Alaska to put you away, any way they can. I would, of course, have to help them since we all know how we get elected." Stimson was pacing in front of Parker. Parker couldn't believe what he was hearing.

"There's big stuff afoot in our state that will put us in the news every day instead of once in a while. The guard is changing, and I'm afraid I won't be with them. They want me out, just like you. Speculation is that there's a group made up of people on all sides of the political post. We think we know who they are, but they have help. I'm telling you this because as soon as you're gone, I'm going in front of the Senate investigators. I'm raw meat and the vultures are hovering. You should look up as well, Parker. The money involved is like no one has ever seen. In fact, I believe our current governor will soon be one of the richest women in the country."

Parker sat in silence. It was as if Stimson wanted the world to know this as his defense. He was beginning to feel sorry for the senator. He was also beginning to feel anxious about his own security.

The conservative radio and newspaper commentators were focusing all of their anger on the governor, while they continually tried to defend Stimson. For the senator to come out and say the opposite, it was more proof of how little people knew in the media and how poorly the reality of politics was delivered to the public.

The senator sat down in a leather chair next to Parker. He reached over and grabbed his forearm just like a scene from *The Godfather*. After taking a deep breath, he began slowly.

"I suggest you find a way out of this. What I'm telling you is that you are a marked man. I survived for years in a different media culture and a different belief about this country. It's beyond our borders now. It's beyond the reality. It's all about instant attention and a wanton disregard for us as a country. The wealthiest people are coming at us with guns blazing to make even more money. They don't care if they make it in China, Borneo, or Vietnam. No matter what happens in America, there is more and more influence from the money people are making in investments. Now it's about the wealthiest people supporting politicians and buying influence like no other time in our history. It makes the pre-Depression 1920s seem like kids' play. This goes right to our health-care system. They follow the money and are sending more and more lobbyists. Their people know that as they become a bigger and bigger part of the GDP and GNP, they get richer as well. For-profit health care will fight to the death anything you bring along. The system you're up against is paying its executives more than God."

Parker continued to sit and stare. He felt as if he was hearing something no one else ever would.

"I'm old, Parker. You aren't." Stimson stood up and straightened his coat. He turned to Parker and extended his hand. "I hope you understand everything, Mr. Moore. I hope you have some influence before you leave." Stimson shook Parker's hand firmly and winked at him. He then extended his left arm out to escort him to the door.

Parker said nothing. He smiled, nodded in appreciation, and turned and walked into the room where the women were enjoying their drinks. He stood momentarily to grasp the situation, knowing he could never repeat any of what he just heard. He wondered what Brooks and Ramsey and whoever else was listening thought.

Stimson shut the door behind him. Months later, he would lose his Senate seat and be found guilty on several counts of ethical charges. All would eventually be dismissed. Two years later, he would be killed in a plane crash. Parker never forgot the conversation. Not a word.

Chapter 60

After the session with Stimson, Parker suspected Stimson knew or was a part of the Super PAC. Parker finished the numbing debriefing with the union reps at a Ruth's Chris Steakhouse dropping all the cash they wanted while they argued about not getting enough pay back home. He awoke the next morning thoroughly convinced his time was up. Stimson knew more about Parker than Parker, which was scary.

He walked over to Lafayette Park and stared at the White House. He wondered if anyone would ever know about his work to ensure the next candidate the most powerful position on Earth. He wondered how many people the NSA had pulled into this exchange to pave the way. He remembered, and smiled about the conversation he had with his graduate school economic professor who was convinced of the theory that only about a half dozen people controlled the country and the world economy. At the time, Parker thought his prof was off his rocker. Now, he thought otherwise.

"Enough!" Parker yelled to himself. He got off the bench and began his usual trek to the Smithsonian. It was time to think about his own evolution and return to his children and a different way of life. He began dialing numbers on his cell phone and told as many good people he made contact with that he was sorry for being so off. He told them about his challenging personal life and how it took the ultimate toll on his professional life. To his surprise, everyone he talked with understood and already knew. Apparently every part of the abusive lifestyle he tried to keep secret was no secret. People wished him well and offered whatever support they could give. Parker stood by the corner of the Treasury Building and quietly sobbed. He was going to disappear and Brooks and Ramsey would just have to find him.

★   ★   ★

The underground office of the NSA was again host to a committee of six; although this time two field personnel joined them. After hearing the latest briefings, the name below Parker's included a strikethrough.

Chapter 61

"**We're done,** Parker," Brooks said. "We don't need you anymore."

"That's it?" Parker replied. His question hid the truth that he knew it was the end and he was glad of it.

"There's not much else to do. I'm sure you know by now your wife is, and has been, living with the investment banker. Your home is rented. Are you almost done with therapy?"

Parker was a little off guard. He kept forgetting these guys knew everything about him.

"I'm not sure," Parker replied as he looked across the Mall at the red-brick turrets of the Smithsonian. He sat back on the bench, stretched out his arms along the top of it, and looked up through the trees. "I don't know," he repeated.

"Have you any idea what you'll do? Stimson's right. They are gunning for you in Alaska, and at this point, we're in no position to help. We can't blow this now. You might just have to be a victim." Brooks was wearing jeans, a t-shirt and a Nationals baseball cap. His dark sunglasses hid his eyes but it seemed he was looking down at Parker as he stood with his arms folded.

"Yes. No. I'm not a victim. I put myself in this mess, and I'll accept what gets me out." Parker was still looking into the trees. "I have a plan."

Brooks looked around, smiling in relief that Parker seemed to understand. He looked toward the Capitol. "You gonna let us in on it?"

"You'll know soon enough, I'm sure."

"You've done some great work, Parker." Brooks swirled dirt with his right shoe. His arms were still crossed. "Maybe there's something we can help you with down the road."

"Maybe." Parker was sitting with his arms and hands between his knees, staring at the ground. "How long will you guys watch me?"

"We'll be around a while. Probably a decision for the people above me, you know. Maybe it depends on what you choose to do."

The financial markets were in ruin. Oil was up to $140 dollars a barrel with gas at the pumps around $4.35 a gallon. Everything the NSA agents told Parker would happen was happening. Two wars were still raging. China's economy was rapidly growing, with India's a close second. The world economy was changing and the players needed to change to bring back some semblance of civility. Stimson knew it.

Parker would have a hand in changing some of the players, but what of the rest? How many others were out there? He knew that very soon his preoccupation with greed, corruption, political and union bribery would end. It was time to face his demons. Parker got up from the bench and looked past Ramsey. He looked up and down the dirt path on the outskirts of the Mall.

"Good luck, Parker," Brooks said. "We may or may not ever see each other again." He shook Parker's hand and began to walk toward the Washington Monument.

Parker watched Brooks for a bit. He flipped him off, smiled, and then sat back down on the bench till evening.

Chapter 62

In Anchorage, Parker looked out the window of his apartment at Mt. Susitna. The Sleeping Lady was dormant, and it was Parker's plan to do the same. He had begun to pack the night before, but now took some time to recall the last few years. It had been a whirlwind. He needed refuge. This time there would be no letter of resignation. He was leaving and not providing any forwarding address or phone number. Keys and ID were already left in his office. He was going to disappear, burn all the bridges, and start over. Sanity and poverty were better than suicide.

As he packed his car to the brim, he planned his route. He knew the Alcan like people knew their neighborhoods. One last look out the window. The tide was coming in to the Cook Inlet; being the second-largest tide in the world, it always made for great viewing. Sometimes even a tidal bore made an appearance. Planes were landing at Elmendorf. Container ships were in port ready to dock, and there were sounds at the Hilton of buses unloading the cruise-ship tourists from Seward. Nothing changed. It would be no different if he were dead or alive. You always hoped the world would stop and take notice of your pain or death, but it didn't.

Parker got in his car, closed the door, and headed for Tok.

Chapter 63

A month later, Parker sat at Dusty's in Okemos. He was thinking about how much his domestic life had been like living with Sharon Stone in *Basic Instinct 2*. Tonight the drink was Dewar's straight. Single malts were too expensive now. He'd just come from what used to be his house. It was as the NSA had told him. Rented to people he didn't know, and they had already trashed the thousands of dollars of work he had done on it. The roses were gone. The lacrosse net gone. Parker Park was gone. He then went to the address he had found for her. A million dollar home and through the window he could see his dining room set. Everything but the car he drove down the Alcan was moved or gone. He left one of the cards in the crack of the front screen door. It was one she'd given him years before. She'd written:

Love you forever

Parker was deep in thought. The Dewar's helped. There was anger at what he had gone through, but he was slowly settling into an acceptance of his responsibility. He chose the career, the wife, and the work with the NSA. Did he feel a victim of domestic violence? Yes. Did he feel a dirty stench covering him from the world of unions and politics? Absolutely. Was there remorse for allowing the NSA to manipulate him into the fold and discover they did nothing but use him? Of course. But in reality, as he finished his sessions with Darryl before he left Alaska, he took responsibility—which is where he'd start now.

"Hey, Moore. Parker Moore. What the hell are you doing here?" It was Jason Truman an old acquaintance from Parker's days hanging around the Capitol Building in Lansing. He was a lobbyist who generally took on small clients for large fees.

"Jason, good to see you." Parker came out of his thoughts and stood up to shake his hand.

"I heard you were thrown out of the business. Cooked, fried, and out with the leftovers."

"Yup. That about sums it up."

"Hey, you see that place your ex's holed up in? The story is you beat her and she was so afraid she started mountin' that banker guy she'd met while … Hey, you knew about this, right?"

"Yes, Jason. I knew about it. And, I did *not* beat her."

"Well, let's just say, I think half the county wishes someone would." Jason looked over at the bartender and ordered a Guinness.

Parker listened to Jason update him about what had been going on with the probable new governor and administration in Michigan. How the corporate world had gotten back at all the unions by sending jobs out of the country, but now the state and country were in hot water because the middle class didn't have any money to buy all the shit made everywhere else. Screwing the unions made for record corporate earnings and a richer upper class, but the economy was crap. Jason droned on about how people were blind to the facts as long as the American Dream was still aired on the dozens of reality shows and tabloid news programs.

After about fifteen minutes, Parker was looking at Jason, nodding and reacting, but he wasn't listening. He ordered another Dewar's with water back and decided to get numb one last time.

Sitting against the window was Blair Donovan, investment banker living with Parker's ex. The two couldn't see each other because of the formation of the bar. Sitting with Blair was Spenser Robinson, another investment guru Parker's ex had slept with for a short while during Parker's days in Chicago. Ice Pick wasn't her only fun. Share and share alike amongst friends they must have figured.

Parker tried not to listen to Jason. A nod of the head and a yes or no once in a while was all it took to keep Jason talking. In the morning, Parker would head to Petoskey for a consulting job. He couldn't wait to get out of Okemos. He had only snuck in to find what he knew was already true.

Chapter 64

The Ending
Michigan—2010

The chest tubes were gone, there was no infection, and Parker was getting ready to go home.

He visualized walking into the house; the tying table just as he had left it with hooks and feathers in mid-tie as a spool of thread hung on the bobbin. Bookshelves lining the walls, along with countless pictures of outdoor adventures, sports, and other memories made the house look like a Hemingway museum. Even the scotch glass aside the various single malts fit the motif of a place where Robert Traver could have written *Anatomy of a Murder*. Toward the front corner was the wood stove surrounded by a wrap-around sofa that always made for a cozy winter night. His blue-leather chair and reading lamp were always at the ready for the next quiet moment.

Outside were three distinct sitting areas. On the front lower patio, rested two chairs protected overhead from a second-floor porch. This was the morning seat to watch the sunrise and an evening perch to watch the shadows travel up the forest across from the house. To the north, four chairs circled the fire ring for late-night laughs and hotdog roasts. Between the two areas was a third spot on a small cement pad that made for the perfect winter rest after snowshoeing. In the winter, the sun stayed here the longest.

With the house surrounded by maple and birch forest, sunlight was precious.

On the north slope, near the house, were bird feeders and bird houses. Parker would often have chickadees feeding out of the palm of his hand.

The serenity of his domain allowed him to heal from the years of political wrangling and the nights of sleeplessness and a mental fatigue only few could imagine. Months of dissociative feelings found him finally seeking help. He made the decision to give everything away, including his career.

In the midst of a Chautauqua community in Northern Michigan, much of his life that had lain dormant for years returned. He found Sam and the circuits seemed complete. Finally, a place for art, music, and literature. Being nestled in his home and surrounded by forest and field, nature became his muse. The strife was over. The chase ended. It had nothing to do with money, night clubs, friends in high places, or being in control of everything.

Parker Moore spent his weeks peacefully now. On Mondays, he'd pick up Irv, a traumatic-brain-injury survivor, and they would head to Brother Dan's food pantry to work for an hour or two. The Monday-night stocking and preparing was for those in need who came during the day on Tuesdays. Tuesday nights were bowling with Henry. A veteran of World War II, Korea, and Vietnam, Henry was eighty-six years old and loved to bowl; Parker enjoyed the evening with Henry at Northern Lights Recreation out on M-119 well before the road turned into the Tunnel of Trees past Harbor Springs along the Lake Michigan coast. Joe, Ed, Tony, or Ellen would make the bowling on Tuesdays perfect as they parlayed their talents and put Henry center stage. On Wednesdays, it was group night at St. Francis. The men's group quenched Parker's thirst for discussion and constant refinement of his spirituality. Every Tuesday, Wednesday and Thursday he worked out with his friend George who was diagnosed with lymphoma and had asked Parker to assist him in regaining his health. On Fridays, Parker volunteered in the Chapel at St. Francis. The weekends were left to Sam and the kids. When all the kids were busy, Sam and Parker kayaked, gardened, played cards, roamed the woods, or just sat and read, but there always seemed to be an adventure somewhere.

Thus, the quiet volunteer life of a man who went at breakneck speed for twenty years. He'd been in one abusive setting after another until he finally realized it was he who kept putting himself in them. He'd been lucky enough to have three amazing and brilliant children, and he'd been able to tour the United States and Canada coast to coast for both career and vacation. Life was a dream, but once the need for constant movement, greater wealth, and prestige took over from the actual desire to just live life as it comes, Parker broke. He simply broke. The balance was lost and he had sold his soul to people who only cared about power and money—both of which Parker never set out to gain. The gain had become what others wanted.

Finally, his political enemies found an opening and destroyed him. It was like taking a wounded horse on the battlefield and watching it writhe before the shot to the head. Parker ended up one of those public figures you see on the front page.

For two years, he secluded himself in a corner of Northern Michigan where he would draw, write, fish, and give everything away instead of only taking or wanting. He was no longer in the business of making others powerful or getting them what they wanted while he killed himself in the process. He devoted himself to this new life. At fifty-two, he re-discovered why, at the age of fifteen, he had wanted to change the world. Best of all, he was off the grid.

He found his self-respect, dignity, and soul. Sam and her community were the icing on the cake. From 3,000 cell-phone minutes a month, and 400 e-mails a day, he sometimes went days without a call or an e-mail. He went to the Roast and Toast for coffee and to play gin with Sam every day. He enjoyed life.

Parker often sat in quiet meditation. He reminisced about the parents of the children he coached over the years, from Little League through high school, and how he loved most of them but argued with a few. He wished he could apologize to all he offended and explain the stress that caused him to say things he would always

188 ★   Stewert James

regret. He remembered the one hockey mom who challenged him about money for the team after Parker had shelled out thousands of his own money just to make the team work. Parker remembered screaming on the phone at her. It had been years since he raised his voice.

Chapter 65

The detective sat in the hospital room listening. Parker was telling his life story for the chance to find the person who shot him. The problem was he had made so many enemies. Parker droned on. His voice grew angry. He thought his life had changed. He thought he was at peace.

The detective looked out the window at the bay. Lake Michigan was cold and black. Winter took a hold early this year. Ice began to layer on the breakwater. Harbor Springs was socked in with a snow squall.

"You know that guy in Illinois? He asked for thousands of dollars, or he wouldn't sign any of our legislation. The senator in Michigan? She wanted ten thousand dollars like she owned us. All the money we had we would divide up equally. Then it was up to me to take the grief and make the board members look good. The entire system is built on bribery and falsity. The scary part? It's so entrenched, it is accepted as the norm."

The detective made notes. Names he thought. Give me names.

"So," he interrupted the diatribe, "why the hell would someone come back and shoot you when everything is over? You're put out to pasture; can't even do the same work anymore, and you expect me to believe they're still out to get you? No offense, but this is really a little farfetched. How about lovers? Scandals?"

"Well, I was married to a borderline."

"A what?"

"A borderline personality. Think of Madonna, Sybil, and the girl in *The Exorcist* all in one body. Make it five-ten, blonde hair, a figure to turn heads, and a smile to get anything she wants. Just don't ever expect anything except drama. Add a little physical abuse, some alcohol, and you've got death in a bikini." Parker stopped and looked out the window. Then he turned back toward the detective. "The problem was I became sicker than she was."

"How long has she been out of your life?"

Parker squirmed and sat up. He didn't like to talk about this. It was painful. He always remembered what she would whisper in his ear or on the phone, "No one will believe you."

"It's been three years, but ..."

"But what?" The detective was losing patience.

"Well, there have been several instances over the last few months of someone being in my house while I was gone. I would literally stop when I walked in the door as if, well, as if someone was watching. As if someone had just left. But there are lots of people who probably would like me dead." Parker straightened himself in bed again. "You know, there was this blonde and group who followed me around Illinois and played nice with the ex-wife. I'm almost positive they were sending Stefanie money."

★   ★   ★

The Petoskey Public Safety Department assigned Tim Johnson the case of the shooting at the Roast and Toast and the homicide. After he interviewed Parker, he sat at his desk to review the files. No fancy room with white boards or multiple computer screens. Just an old wooden desk and a chair. The same gun was involved in the murder on Emmet Street blocks away from the shooting at the coffee shop. No witnesses. No connected motives. His interview with Parker Moore offered several leads that needed to be checked out, including a violent, angry woman who looked great in a bikini and supposedly became a crack shot with a .357. *Yeah right,* he thought. *None of it made sense. Political enemies didn't shoot people—at least not in this small corner of the world, and especially not in Petoskey.*

The photo of the dead man was not recognized by the staff or customers in the Roast and Toast, or anywhere else Johnson asked. The body was found by the landlord looking to collect the rent. He didn't know anything about the guy other than he always paid on time. It was interesting that the tenant had the landlord pick up the rent and it was always in cash. One bullet through the head. Dead on impact. *Some flimsy blonde make that shot?* The case just didn't fly, but a call was warranted to cover all the bases.

Chapter 66

The detective had left and it was Parker's turn to look out the window. The squall was gone and the lights of Harbor Springs, Boyne Highlands, and Nub's lit up the night sky. Parker's home sat west of the Highlands. He reached deep into his synapses and thought.

He would walk into his house and stop without even shutting the door. "Someone has been here," he whispered to himself. "Everything looks okay." But Parker felt an energy; an aura of a person having walked through his space. He never locked the doors because it felt good not to, and he didn't think anyone would ever come down his road. It was a dead-end and he had virtually nothing of value. Still, he was convinced someone had been in the house; it happened more than once.

As he reflected on the last few months, his jaws began to tighten. The fear he believed to be gone returned. He hadn't even realized that he had felt a sense of being watched. It didn't matter that he'd begun to lock his door. The sense of being stalked wouldn't leave. *Who would do it and why?* The why was probably easier than the who, but all was over, decided, and done. His past was his past, and as public as it was, it was settled.

He traced his memory for people like Ice Pick who might still hold grudges. There was a meeting at Dusty's in Okemos years ago.

There was no one in the restaurant except for himself, the Michigan governor's power broker, the bartender, and a waitress. It was late, and the Lagavulin was warm. The gentleman from the governor's office motioned to the two employees and they left the room. He was in a black suit and red tie staring at Parker. He held his gin with his right hand while he ran the index finger of his left hand around the rim. His elbows rested on the table. He stared at the glass as he began to talk.

"What I'm saying is, if you don't give us any trouble, we'll take care of things."

Parker sat back in his chair, wanting to smile, but remained stoic. He kept imagining he was in some Dashiell Hammett novel and Sam Spade was about to enter the room. He wanted to imitate Humphrey Bogart and had to stop himself from pursing his lips.

"Okay," Parker said, "but we will be at odds on some things."

"We know that, but it's all part of the public game. You get your licks in and we get ours in. The public stays status quo with both sides, and we know that the end game is already in the bag. If we get too cozy, certain moneyed constituents won't be happy. But, if you fuck with us, you get nothing."

The governor of Michigan ran the state like a well-oiled, multinational company. He had even given titles to his directors like a private business would. There were CEOs and COOs holding public offices, and the accoutrements to go along with their titles. Most of all, you could never get to the governor. He always had someone for you to go through, no matter the circumstance.

Parker had always dreamed of being in the inner circle. He'd have a noble social notion of being able to do the right thing for the right cause. As he learned, the right cause only went with how many votes you could obtain or how much money you could raise. Unless something hit the front pages with a big splash, the state government simply worked through individual needs and mostly on the budget. The budget was everything. Hundreds of thousands of people could be affected if Parker was to tell the governor's man to fuck off. He learned quickly to pick his battles and wait.

"No problem, Ed. We'll keep it civil and anything else I can do personally, you just let me know." Parker swirled his scotch in the snifter as he stared across the table watching for any hint of emotion.

"Agreed."

With a final sip of gin, the governor's man slid the check folder toward Parker and winked. Politics. Who paid the bill and who controlled the power didn't always equate to the same person.

Chapter 67

Parker continued to wonder about enemies he made in the past. He continued to work on some connectivity to it all. As if someone or some group used him when he never even realized it. Years ago after that meeting in Dusty's with the Governor of Michigan's right-hand man, the governor needed him again.

"Parker? I'm on a cell phone. When I get to a secure line, I'll call you. Be in your office within the hour." Ed hung up.

Parker was almost to his office. He shook his head when the line was disconnected.

Once he got to his office, he settled into his chair and turned his computer on. His secretary, Pam, poked her head in.

"Ed's on the phone. He said you'd know what it was about." She rolled her eyes and went back to her desk.

"Parker, we have a problem with one of our senators. He's a good party man and chairs one of our most important committees, but he's a drunk. He's screwing up energy policy for the governor and the entire way we set pricing standards for the utilities. Worst of all, this could lose the governor some votes." Ed was matter of fact, but his tone was angry.

"Okay." Parker was looking over his mail and settling into his office as he listened. "And you need an intervention?"

"Yes. With your experience, you're the only one we know who can do it." Ed was serious; his tone was low, and challenging.

Until then, Parker hadn't lost a piece of legislation. He had drafted the legislative language and written the business plan for the company that eventually had oversight over all impaired health professionals in the state. The thoracic surgeons who stopped drinking just long enough to operate; the nurses who gave themselves more Demerol than their patients; the dentists who had white powder under their noses as they pointed a drill in someone's mouth. The hundreds of professionals the public and the state government didn't want to know existed. Just fix them, was the job. According to state and federal law, once in the system and assuming compliance, the professional's problems were confidential to everyone. Even the Drug Enforcement Agency (DEA) tried to crack the system. Parker smiled when he thought of the two practitioners still working today, sober. They had no idea how close they came to losing everything. They never harmed a patient and continued to have excellent practices. They would never know Parker was responsible for their well-being today. They were using so many drugs the DEA was convinced they were selling and dealing. Three agents visited Parker at the unmarked and out-of-sight offices, but the agents left empty-handed. No court order, no information.

The intervention Ed was asking for was like any other intervention except this one was going to be in the State Senate Hearing Room with the floor shut down by the State Police, and a detective in the ante room with a breathalyzer.

All the VIPs were at the table when Ed escorted the senator into the room. Everyone was seated, and the men began to tell the senator how much they admired him and how much they respected him, but how much they wished he'd get help. One by one each person gave objective detail about what people saw, what events were out of place, and what the future may hold. The senator listened as if he was in a room of constituents. His hands were folded in front of him and he looked into each man's eyes as he heard their stories. He would nod and say yes, but the sweat was beading and then dripping off of his forehead. His hands began to shake. The rancid odor of a late-stage alcoholic's breath needing a drink was strong in the room. Arrangements were made for a hospital detoxification bed, and transportation was ready as soon as the intervention was over. If the senator refused and attempted to drive away, the breathalyzer was at the ready.

After everyone left the room, the senator, now blurry eyed and breathing faster, slowly stood up. He looked at Parker.

"You son of a bitch. I'm going nowhere, and you will pay for this someday. Mark my words. You will pay." He went out of the committee room and into his private office. Parker followed him.

"Senator, you have a choice. Go to treatment and keep your committee seat, or as soon as you try to drive off, you'll be arrested for impaired driving and on the front pages tomorrow." Parker was standing in front of the senator's desk, staring into the man's bulging, angry eyes.

"Go to hell!" the senator yelled as he tried to light a cigarette. His hands were shaking so much he couldn't do it.

"Senator?"

He threw the lighter against the wall, grabbed his coat, and headed toward the door. He stopped.

"Who's taking me?" He was looking at the floor trying to catch his breath. One hand held the door while the other was at his side with a clenched fist.

"They're outside in a black Lincoln. It's someone you'll recognize, someone who went through the same thing."

"Don't ever expect anything from me." The senator slammed the door behind him.

He would spend a week in detox, two weeks in treatment, and months later have a grand mal seizure on the floor of the Senate. His wife didn't agree with the intervention and never helped him stop drinking. His political career was finished. He never stopped threatening Parker.

Chapter 68

Parker opened his eyes. He sat up in the hospital bed startled at 3:00 a.m. He felt around the bed and made sure he was in the present. Eyes wide open, his preoccupation shifted to the night before the shooting.

The Center City Gym was on Mitchell Street near the center of downtown Petoskey. It was a standard gym without the fancy fluff. It was for body builders and people who didn't care if the locker room didn't smell like lavender. Parker loved his workouts and had a cadre of friends he saw each day while lifting weights.

As usual, Paul was on the treadmill around 4:30 p.m. while George and Parker sat directly behind on the recumbent bikes. All three were warming up before the heavy lifting began. The favorite TV show this month was reruns of *The Andy Griffith Show*. Barney was yelling about Otis in this particular scene.

"I think someone's been trying to get in my locker," Parker said.

"Shush. This is hysterical." George wouldn't look at Parker. He just held his hand up and kept watching the TV.

"No, really. Three days in a row my shoes were moved, and that's where I keep my key."

Paul and George both laughed.

"Well, duh, maybe you shouldn't keep your key in the shoe anymore," Paul said.

"I know. I know. I have it right here now. But I'm tellin' ya. My locker, my house, hell, even the door of my car was ajar the other day when I came out of Glen's Market." His anxiety was growing, even after two years away from Alaska.

"If it's about someone being after you again, forget it. We don't want to hear it. Everything is over, Parker. You're a nobody; just like you wanted." George smiled and looked forward to watching Otis walk into the Mayberry jail, open up the cell, and put the keys back on the wall.

After an hour, the workout was over. George and Paul were talking at the top of the stairs. Parker headed down to the locker room. As he turned the corner by the last weight machine, a person he'd never seen before came running out of the locker room. He ran into Parker.

"Sorry. Excuse me." The stranger ran up the stairs.

Parker continued into the locker room. He stopped dead in his tracks. His locker was wide open.

Chapter 69

The DEA had an informant in Petoskey they used to track shipments and sales of different drugs in Emmet County; especially in Bay Harbor and Harbor Springs. People with money, young and old, used drugs. They could afford it and usually maintained a high-functioning life while rationalizing their use.

In any case, the informant had been useful in other parts of the country; he was originally part of the Miami scene. Vic suggested him to Ramsey and Brooks when they found Parker living in Harbor Springs. As an informant, Perry received a steady flow of cash as long as he produced and stayed sober. And the work kept him out of prison after his trouble with cocaine. His one weakness? Women.

Perry hadn't been fully briefed yet by Brooks. There was just a short conversation when they shared a beer in Vanderbilt at the Ugly Bar. He moved into a house on Emmet Street in the old district of Petoskey. Perry filled his fridge with favorites, but was careful to not make any aesthetic changes to the house. He did keep a supply of wine just in case he brought a woman home. His favorite pastime was sipping club sodas at Papa Lou's. He never worried about road-testing his sobriety.

It was a Wednesday night when she walked in. She was easy to spot. Over six feet tall in stiletto heels and an aloofness that turned men on. She ordered a Cosmo as she sat next to Perry. Four hours later, she was at Perry's house with nothing between them but a bed sheet. Sometime during the early morning hours she left—but not before Perry made the mistake of giving her his pre-paid cell phone number. She sent him a text:

Thanks. I needed that.

Perry tried to call her a few times, but she never answered the phone. The next time he saw her was on a Saturday morning as he was walking toward the Roast and Toast. He was rounding the corner in the park near City Park Grill after finishing his workout at Center City Gym. He'd joined as a member to keep close track of Parker Moore. He almost got caught getting into Parker's locker, but never while snooping in his house. Perry never took anything. He did get very good at tracking and giving information to his handlers. Since the meeting with Brooks, he wanted to keep making a good impression, and if it made Vic happy, it was all good.

★   ★   ★

Before she left Perry's, just days before the shooting, she noticed a scribbled note on his counter. A note Perry wasn't supposed to write:

Parker Moore
6921 State Road
Harbor Springs
NSA Brooks

She grabbed her phone and entered the address. "NSA? Well hellloooo," she said quietly with a grin.

Over the last two years, she had tracked Parker north and planned her attack, but then he'd moved and was off the grid. After finding his new place, it took her too long to look around town and wait trip after trip north to find him. She knew his habits and wanted to see his house. She made a visit during the day, careful in her approach. Since it was winter, there was hardly a person ever back by Parker's. He also left his door unlocked, so getting in was easy. The first thing she spotted was a fleece she'd given him hanging by the door. Parker had given everything back to her except that fleece.

"Asshole," she said out loud as she smiled and shook her head. She grabbed the fleece as she looked around.

★　★　★

After the shooting at the Roast and Toast, Brooks couldn't find Perry. He went to the address on Emmet Street the DEA had given him. He found Perry, dead. One shot to the forehead. Brooks looked around to see what he needed to clean up and to figure out how the man supposed to keep an eye on Parker Moore ended up dead. Neither the landlord nor the police had found the body yet.

Who the hell would take this guy out, and why? The only thing Brooks knew about Perry was that he chased the ladies and often got chastised by the DEA for jeopardizing covers.

Brooks had entered the house with his gloves on, so he picked up the cell phone on the floor and perused the numbers. Brooks' number wasn't there because they used runners or couriers. Brooks copied the numbers and put the phone back where he had found it. He recognized the numbers and decided it might help down the road if the local police saw them and eventually figured out who they belonged to.

The only other item he found was a note with Parker Moore's address lying on the counter, a note Perry wasn't supposed to write.

Brooks took several pictures of the layout and what was in the house. Leaving the scene as it was, he walked out the back door and came around to Sheridan. He walked past the Road Commission garages, the community garden, and eventually entered the parking lot at Glen's Market south where he got into his car. His small, gray Buick was nondescript, and as far as he could tell, no one gave any attention to him.

He got on his encrypted cell phone and made a call. A woman picked up the phone. After a short conversation, she left her office and drove north on US-23 then eastbound on I-96 in her gray Buick. Brooks never had to call her again. It was a job that should have been done three years ago, but the elimination of a subject was always hard. Especially one with kids.

★   ★   ★

In Okemos, Blair sat in the waiting room. His attorney was an hour late. After being released from jail, Blair needed a place to stay. He had asked his attorney for a ride to a friend's house in Haslet. This guy had dated Stefanie for a short time—Blair never knew if it was another one of her affairs or if she was in-between husbands at the time. All he knew was this man was sympathetic to his situation. And it was better than the Red Roof Inn and not too close to her work.

★   ★   ★

After the deputies left her house, she had taken a long, hot bath. The tub had jets but the warmth of the water was enough. She wondered if Parker was dead. She hoped Blair would just go away and leave her everything. Her first husband wouldn't do that. In fact, he moved in next door for a few years till she moved out. Those were the years with Parker. Her kids could come and go as they pleased, while Parker's children lived an hour away. She would throw fits to prevent him from going to visit them and then leave to see her lover while Parker stewed. *He was such a coward.*

The house was cold and quiet. Stefanie never heard or saw the gray Buick in front of the house. With no streetlights it was the perfect place to park just short of the cul-de-sac. The window of the car opened just enough to let the cigarette smoke billow out.

★   ★   ★

Detective Tim Johnson walked around the Roast and Toast that night and then up Emmet Street. What connected the two shootings besides the bullet? Who could come into a town or be in a town and no one see him? Him? Maybe no one would look for a woman. No witnesses. The director was ready to release all of the info. A press conference would be held later in the morning. As Petoskey slept, Detective Johnson walked and wondered.

Johnson tried to probe deeper into the dead man's life. Nothing. His fingerprints were gone; there was only scar tissue. Dental records were only good if they knew where he had lived. Nothing matched in the databases or with local dentists. There was no ID. Nothing except a pre-paid cell phone with twelve recent calls. Six in and six out. No local numbers. There were a few items of clothing and groceries; different than expected. It was all specialty food from the Grain Train and some pretty expensive meat from Tannery Creek. There was some cash in the house, a few hundred dollars in various bills, so the guy could afford it. Some wine too; mostly high-end cabernets and pinots, not what you'd expect from someone living in a home that looked the way this one did.

The crime scene was too clean. Just the body and blood. No other prints and no shell casing.

Chapter 70

Conclusion

"**Gentleman, now** that the decision we all feared has been cast in stone, we must move quickly. Citizen's United has created a rapid movement of chatter and activity aligning money and power in places far worse than the union halls of the 1930's and the corporate boardrooms of the 1990's. Our work in several states has been successful; so far the media hasn't reached us or the people working for us. Governors are gone. Legislators are gone. But there remains one problem in Michigan. I'm afraid our elimination order was delayed."

The Director of the Super PAC stopped pacing and stood directly behind John Mansfield.

"Ma'am it wasn't delayed in the way you—" he started.

"Oh, I understand," she interrupted as she placed her hands on Mansfield's shoulders. The director looked around the table at the five other members. "Killing someone is difficult; killing someone who has the responsibility of children and a family is not usually our goal—but in this instance, the danger is great since this person has a connection to groups we just worked to clean up; groups with the potential for much influence. It is time."

"The call was made ma'am. It will happen soon."

"Thank you, Mr. Mansfield. That will be all gentlemen."

★   ★   ★

"More?" Sam asked. It was a warm day in early March 2010. Parker was home from the hospital.

"Yes, please," Parker said as he sat staring across the front yard. It felt good to be home and outside on the porch.

Sam poured Lagavulin in the crystal glass Parker received as a gift from his daughter, Julie.

"So, what do you think?" she asked as she poured a little more pinot into her glass.

"I think someone's been in the house. My fleece is gone ... I know someone's been in here." Parker's voice was angry, mostly from fear. He was more confident every day but couldn't get away from the anxiety that he'd walk into his house and meet a bullet before he could reach for a light switch.

The scotch was smooth. A slow warmth made Parker close his eyes only to remember all the single malts with Stefanie as she drank her Cosmos. Mind erasers she called them. Sex would happen in the car or on the road before they reached the house.

"Parker? Parker? Hello, I'm here—not her." Sam smiled but she was getting tired of the whole preoccupation thing.

"Yeah, Sam. I'm here. I just need to get over this."

He slipped back into the past. A couple hundred dollars every Friday was all it took. The train rides and the drives from Chicago were long and arduous, but it never mattered to Stefanie. All she wanted was a night out and a weekend of fun. Parker's sixty- to eighty-hour work week made a weekend of sex and fun easy. The house was looking better and the five acres was becoming a sanctuary. Didn't matter. There was always the threat of violence. The property she secretly purchased in Toledo. Late nights at the Green Door. Dates with men who had money. Parker had taken care of her children and rebuilt her life, but it was never enough.

"Do you think it's her?" Sam asked as she gazed across the cornfield.

"Her who? What?" Sam's question broke Parker from his reverie.

"Do you think she's getting into the house?" Sam looked at Parker.

"Yes. I think it's her but I can't prove it," he said as he looked out at the field.

"I think you should move in with me." Sam was swirling her wine.

"I would love to. When I'm ready. I need to finish this." Parker sipped his scotch.

"Parker, you've faced everything. The kids, the courts, your professional life, now this. What else?" Sam was becoming more frustrated.

"It has to go away." Parker turned to her and gently brushed her cheek with the back of his hand.

Another sip of scotch, and the warmth returned. Parker shut his eyes.

Chapter 71

The Ingham County Sheriff's office was quiet when the call came in. Football season at MSU was over and basketball season hadn't yet reached March Madness; the only student activity to prepare for was St. Patrick's Day.

"Sergeant Jones." Max Jones was a twenty-year veteran of the department. He had settled into a nice niche and only had a few years left before retirement. Born and bred in Wheatfield Township, he still maintained his family's centennial farm on Meridian Road.

"Hello, Sergeant. This is Detective Tim Johnson with Petoskey Public Safety. How are you?"

"Fine, sir. Fine. How can I help you?" Jones replied in a monotone.

"I'm investigating a shooting. Well, two actually. One is a homicide. The other one, well the victim says he is connected with a woman in Okemos. She has a history of domestic violence and she is not always the victim," Johnson began.

"Yes, continue." Jones was glancing at the *Lansing Journal* while he listened.

"Well, it's a long shot but I wondered ..."

As Johnson droned on about his case, Jones was thinking about his last night at Omar's. The local strip joint wasn't where police officers should hang out, but Jones made it a habit. What made it more intriguing for the sergeant was that Omar's was only a block from the State Capitol on Michigan Avenue. He'd often see people who didn't want to be seen there, and if they saw him, it became instant approval. No one told anyone. Jones wasn't married, so what did he care? It was a public place for anyone to visit, and he liked dating the girls.

"… anyway, I was wondering if there were any recent domestic issues related to this woman." Johnson had finished.

Jones gathered his attention. He asked for her name and typed it into the computer.

"Well, whadda ya know? There was a guy brought in a few months back who claimed he was a victim while being arrested as the perp. It was a he-said-she-said case. Anyway …"

As Johnson listened and took notes, he thought about his dinner the night before at the Palette Bistro where he and his wife celebrated their tenth wedding anniversary. Johnson's life was altogether different than Jones'.

"Wait. What was that?" Johnson suddenly came back to the call.

"Yeah, he said she hit him. That she launched herself down the stairs and is now filing for divorce and wants everything he owns." Jones seemed interested now.

"Can I have her address?"

"Sure."

Chapter 72

Sam got up the next morning and looked outside at the sunrise over the hillside. The coffee was strong and the warmth of the sun was comforting. She'd been through her own torment, but why try to kill someone years later? What would drive someone to such a degree?

Peaceful, yet shrouded in mystery, Parker snored softly in the bedroom.

★　★　★

In Okemos, Stefanie got out of bed and looked outside. The Buick was gone from out front; she never knew it was there. Kids were still asleep and Blair was in Haslet. *Good*, she thought. This would all be hers when done. His stock market portfolio was going through ups and downs only a saint could live through. All of his investment clients bailed when his company was bought out, and he lost his vice presidency. She didn't leave him like the others since he had the right assets. She slipped on her silk sleep-shirt and wandered downstairs.

The coffee was ready as programmed and the kids' soccer tournament didn't start for a few hours. She looked out the back window at the sprawling grounds and wondered how Parker's family might be doing. The shot was perfect—she had practiced for months at the shooting range. The range time was free, except for whatever sex she provided to the owner.

She filled a coffee mug and returned her thoughts to Blair. Her lawyer was pretty confident she'd land the house and whatever she wanted. After two other marriages, and this one, she was accumulating a decent life for a secretary. The wealthiest clerical staff in East Lansing! She smiled as she blew gently into the coffee mug before her first sip.

Through the years growing up in a small town, she felt the wrath of her peers when they made fun of her mother cleaning houses. She watched as her father's business dried up, and they lost their home. The sexual abuse from her grandfather ... it all played a part in the development of the personality that now haunted everyone she got close to. Her affect soured from the smile as she continued to feel the past. *I'll show 'em*, she thought. The moods fluctuated continually throughout the day. The more stress, the more they'd flux. She sipped the hot coffee without blowing. The pain from the heat was a comfort. She actually didn't feel it. In fact, all pain felt good. It kept the bad feelings at bay. When they would crop up, she'd rationalize about her life. No need for college loans or writing term papers. She just needed to keep her looks.

She walked onto the back deck and settled into the wicker lounge chair and smiled.

Chapter 73

Johnson sauntered into the director's office. "Sir," he said as he looked down at some papers in his hand. "I think we have a lead on the Roast and Toast shooting. Still can't piece the puzzle over to the Emmet Street murder, even though we know it's the same weapon. We've spent a couple months checking out the rest of Moore's past."

"Okay?" The director did not look up from his desk. "It's about fucking time. I'd like to retire this year with this solved, Johnson."

"It's a domestic-violence queen who seems to be turning into a black widow. She perpetrates the violence then takes advantage of the typical male response. Two of her husbands hit her, but our guy didn't. But, she did take all of his money and set him up for a huge personal and professional fall. He thinks she may have come after him. Again, the Emmet Street victim—no clue how he fits in until we talk to her. The only evidence is the pre-paid cell phone we found on the premises showing a text to a 517 number that coincidentally is the same number as our black widow."

The director looked up as Johnson progressed through his theory. He clasped his hands behind his head and sat back in his chair. "Can't really arrest her or have her picked up yet. You ready to make a little road trip?"

"Sure. Wife's going out of town for a week or so to Marquette. Works for me."

"Good. Make a call and arrange to question her once you get there. See what turns up. Anything else from Moore?"

"The guy's mysterious." Johnson was turning to leave the office when the director asked the question. He stopped, grabbed the door jamb, and turned halfway around and shook his head while answering. "His history is pretty public, but he claims there are parts that aren't. Some wild stuff about working with federal agents that we find no history of—but I will say this, every place he's been there's a connection to public officials in pretty high places being rocked. There are people in Michigan who have threatened him. He even says someone followed him around Illinois trying to blackmail him, and then someone tried to kill him in Anchorage. Again, no record. The shooting was in the paper but he's not mentioned. It's like he just fell out of the sky and landed in Harbor Springs."

"So, he's done nothing here we care about except get shot. Let me know what you find from the woman." The director went back to his papers.

"You got it, Chief," Johnson yelled over his shoulder as he walked away.

Chapter 74

Parker got up and walked downstairs. The sun was strong through the windows. He kissed Sam on the neck as she sat in the chair on the porch.

"Morning, doll."

"Morning." Sam looked up with a smile. She had both her hands around the coffee cup. Her legs sideways up under her in the chair.

"All good?" Parker was whistling.

"Yes." Sam was contemplative.

"I feel really good this morning." Parker looked out over the fields to the forest. The snow pack was still high.

"I'm glad. Parker? Have you decided what you're going to do next? I mean, you're settling in again, working a little, painting a little, writing a little, but what next?"

Parker sipped his coffee as he leaned against a pillar. "I'm going to forgive and finally let go. In the realms of personality disorders, the more you hang on and the more you communicate with them, you give them all the power. The only thing I want to do is go downstate, say 'I forgive you,' and turn around and leave without an answer."

"Forgive? Forgive?" Sam was standing. "A person who ruins your life, beats you, and now maybe tries to kill you … forgive? You're …" Sam caught herself. She quickly remembered her own issues with domestic violence and how she gave everything away to escape. "Okay. Okay. Maybe you're right. Then, we can move on."

"The police can figure it out. I'm through with the fear. I'm through with the shit. It's a past that keeps rearing its ugly head, and I want it gone." Parker was confident in his stance.

"How then? I mean, how do you pull this off? You know she's probably living like you never existed and will laugh at you after she screams at you because she will never take responsibility. You are returning power to her just by showing up." Sam pressed her point with a softer voice.

"Well, I think we should go down, walk up to her door, and when she answers I'll say 'I forgive you,' and walk away, never to be seen again." Parker was like a child talking about a bad parent.

"I have to hand it to you, Parker. It sounds crazy, but maybe you can get piece of mind. I agree with the concept, but this woman isn't your average normal person." Sam was sitting again and looking up at Parker. Her hand was covering her eyes from the bright sun. In early March, there weren't any leaves so the sun was glaring. "Don't expect me to be nice."

"Doll, you don't even have to get out of the car."

★   ★   ★

The Buick followed her to the soccer tournament. Someone driving a black Benz never worried about a Buick. The only gaze would go to a car that might have cost more than a Benz. She dropped off two kids at the indoor soccer field off Jolly Road then went to the Quality Dairy to get coffee. Speedway was her favorite, but it was too far to drive before the games started.

★   ★   ★

Blair sat at the coffee shop on Main Street across from the theater. He watched people come and go from the McDonald's next door. Slowest McDonald's in the country. It was known for its slow food. He remembered watching her when she was married to Parker. He'd look at her and notice her beauty. Her sultry swagger and long legs. A few times, Blair could tell they'd been fighting, but little did he know who was actually the cause.

Blair's coffee was steaming and strong. He blew on it before taking a sip and wondered how he could have been so stupid. He was willing to give up the house as long as he could keep his investments. She'd already stolen money, property, and retirement from two men, and they'd ended up in trouble with the law too. Through it all, she kept rolling and her kids kept busy. In fact, so busy with sports and school and their social lives they didn't really feel anything. It's like they didn't exist.

Another drink of coffee before the bagel.

Blair's job had changed. He had given up everything for her. He shook his head and stared at the coffee.

He took a large gulp now that it was cooled.

Do you get even or do you let it go? His lawyer suggested a no-contact clause in the agreement and that Blair take his money and run as far away as possible. Blair had two previous marriages and two sets of kids living nearby, so he couldn't run far. He smiled an angry smile and wondered how the other two dupes were doing. Oh, how she and he would sit around making fun of them.

He pushed himself away from the counter and thought about going to the Exchange Nightclub one more time. She'd be there on a Friday night. Maybe he would get one last look at her.

Chapter 75

Johnson obtained a search warrant from the judge and made arrangements with Jones in Ingham County to assist. He'd drive down on Friday and scope the area out. Jones invited him to dinner while in town. Johnson, having not been to Lansing for years, figured he'd make a weekend out of it. They'd serve the warrant on Sunday, and he'd be home that night or Monday at the latest.

★   ★   ★

Parker and Sam left Thursday. Road trips were fun with music, food, and anything else that came from a spontaneity that only the sincere love they had for each other could hatch.

★   ★   ★

Stefanie sat at work, opening mail. Green-and-white paraphernalia filled the office. MSU's sports teams were back in the tank and the trademark revenue was down. Good thing she'd amassed a fortune from three men. The university was threatening layoffs. A smile came to her face as she thought about the Exchange Nightclub on Friday. A young kid from Boston had been hanging around. He was some big shot from Nike's East Coast division. She had him hooked.

★   ★   ★

The Buick sat on Abbot across from the Union; its driver watching who came and left the building. Before the end of the workday it was gone. The Buick left Lansing and headed toward Stockbridge on M-52 and then to Ann Arbor. It parked near the federal building on Washington Avenue.

Chapter 76

Johnson checked into the Hampton Inn off I-96 and Okemos Road on Friday afternoon. He called Jones for the night's plans. The Ingham detective thought Omar's might be the place to take a small-town cop from Petoskey. Plus, it was Friday and his girlfriend was dancing.

★   ★   ★

Parker and Sam checked into the Radisson in downtown Lansing at Grand and Michigan. It was two blocks from the Capitol and one block from the Exchange. Parker thought it would help with his journey to enter an old haunt with Sam and enjoy himself. Sam was always up for dancing.

★   ★   ★

Blair kept himself busy at the office. Some clients changed their portfolios, and he called in their changes along with the normal e-mail. It took his mind off the preoccupation of going out that night. A couple came in for some premarital advice about combining financial assets. He thought about his recent situation and wanted to scream at them to go their separate ways, but he listened and offered the best advice he could under the circumstances. He kept looking at his watch and checking his BlackBerry and e-mail for messages but there were none. Time was dragging. He wondered about his infatuation of waiting for a message he would never get, and the emotional power she had over him. Blair was nervous about facing someone he'd rather see dead. *Who would she be with?* Not *if* she'd be with someone, but *who*.

★　★　★

She quit work early and left the Union at 3:00 p.m. She went home to change. As she laid out her two-hundred-dollar jeans, three-hundred-dollar Dolci and Gabana top, along with her very favorite silver-chained G-string, she sipped vodka and cranberry juice. Grey Goose was her new favorite. The kids were with their dad. She had a whole weekend planned for the kid from Boston. *Why not?* She'd never see him again.

It was a pleasant March evening. The snow was gone in Lansing and the breeze coming out of the southwest was warm. Rain was in the forecast, but a special night at the Exchange was awaiting all. No cover charge and two-for-one drink specials since the legislators were getting ready for spring break.

★　★　★

Johnson and Jones finished their burgers at the Nuthouse before heading over to Omar's. Johnson wasn't sure what he was getting into, but he and Jones hit it off pretty well, and Johnson hadn't been out for a night like this in the ten years he'd been married. There was talk in Petoskey of Johnson being next in line for the Director of Public Safety. If he got that position, there definitely wouldn't be any more nights like this one.

★ ★ ★

Parker and Sam were enjoying a glass of wine at the bar on the lower level of the Radisson. Sam was excited to go dancing. She knew they were going to a nightclub Parker used to frequent. However, dancing didn't come very often in Sam's busy life—it made for a romantic evening.

Chapter 77

The Buick, which had returned from Ann Arbor, followed the black Benz north to Grand River Avenue. They both turned west toward Okemos. The Meridian Mall traffic was light so following was easy. As they traveled past East Lansing, no one would suspect anything of the two cars. They both parked on Michigan Avenue in front of the Lansing Expo Center across from the Exchange. She exited the Benz, ran across the street, and into the nightclub. The cracked window of the Buick let the cigarette smoke curl out and into the soft breeze.

* * *

Soon after entering the club, she reappeared with the young man from Boston, They walked next door to Omar's. As they entered, Johnson held the door for them; he and Jones were just arriving. Johnson thought how cool it was to have a gorgeous blonde pulling a guy half her age into a strip club. He smiled and shook his head as he looked down at the carpet leading inside.

* * *

Parker and Sam decided to drive the short distance since rain was in the forecast. They crossed Michigan Avenue and drove toward the Exchange, parking on the south side of the street. As they walked into the club, Parker noticed the Buick. It looked familiar and he felt unease; then he dismissed it as a paranoid thought. Just a passing memory.

★　★　★

Blair parked his Rendezvous in the lot behind the Exchange. He walked up the back stairs and into the club.

★　★　★

Johnson and Jones were sitting at the downstairs bar at Omar's watching Jones' current squeeze show her stuff on the pole. The conversation between the two men ranged from differences between their two locales, crooks, and the ways women danced. Like most other people in the bar, Johnson would only glance at the dancer. He'd try to sneak a peek without staring, while Jones glared. Then there were men around the stage who could care less about what anyone thought. Johnson noticed the woman with the young kid at a table. He was drinking a beer. Looked like a Guinness. She had a Cosmo of some kind that showed pink through the martini glass. It fit her. The two were no more than a couple inches apart with her tattered designer jeans showing each curve she had; her eyes never left her partner's. A dancer came by, and she whispered something in the dancer's ear. The dancer left with a nod and went up the staircase. She grabbed the young man by the collar and whispered in his ear. He smiled and both of them bolted up the staircase to the private tables.

"Wow," Johnson mumbled to himself. He just couldn't stop thinking about that couple. That stuff didn't happen in Petoskey.

★   ★   ★

Parker and Sam had hung their coats on bar chairs and were already dancing to "Mustang Sally." The dance floor was packed with baby boomers.

Blair was sipping a martini and watching the crowd. The Exchange was a popular hangout for singles, swingers, and anyone else who wanted to get lucky. He saw Parker and Sam and recognized Parker immediately. Blair actually stood up from his seat at a back high-table and stared.

"That son of a bitch, what's he doing here?" he said in an angry whisper. "Well, he's not with her at least." He sat down.

He didn't feel as angry as he would have imagined, and actually wondered about similar experiences she would have had with Parker.

★   ★   ★

The Buick turned around and was now parked on the same side of the street as the Exchange but about one hundred feet west of the main entrance.

Chapter 78

The Nike rep was in disbelief. The dancer was slowly gyrating to the music and bending down in his face so her breasts were as close as they could be to his mouth without actually touching. His newfound friend from MSU was sitting next to him, kissing his ear, and rubbing the inside of his thigh. Boston was home, but this was heaven.

Johnson and Jones were finishing their third beers and now faced the dance floor. Johnson figured it was time to join in the fun.

★ ★ ★

Michigan Avenue was a wide street that ran east-west. It handled the heavy daily traffic to the Capitol and the Expo Center, plus people attending the Lansing Lugnut games at Oldsmobile Park. At night, once the clubs were full, the traffic lessened. A light rain began to fall; so no one was outside. The smokers were relegated to the rear of the clubs since congregating in front was bad for business.

★ ★ ★

"How are you feeling, Parker?" Sam wondered.

The band was on a break and there was quiet music playing in the background

"Good. Really good. In fact, I can't tell you how …" he looked to the rear and saw Blair. He'd only seen Blair once, but Parker was pretty sure it was him.

"What's wrong?" Sam asked as she turned to follow Parker's gaze.

"Well, I think that's her new guy."

"Who? Where?" Sam looked like she was sitting on a top as she spun around.

"Stop! Cripe. Don't look. He's sitting behind you and to your left at the back high-table. Black hair and drinking a martini."

"Well, shit. I'll just head to the bathroom and smile at him, how's that?" Sam was playing, but she was getting tired of this drama. She stood up, kissed Parker on the cheek, turned, and walked toward Blair. As she neared his table, Blair suddenly got very interested in his martini and BlackBerry. After passing him, Sam turned to Parker, put her hands up next to her ears, waved, and stuck out her tongue at Blair.

"Yeah. That's right. You tell 'em honey," Parker said quietly as he smiled. "Unbelievable."

Chapter 79

The kid from Boston was sloshed after his fifth tequila shot and fourth lap dance. They'd talked about anything shallow, giggled like a couple high school kids, and watched everyone watching them. His shirt was unbuttoned down to his navel, hair mussed, and eyes bloodshot.

"Whaddya think about getting outta here?" she asked. After four cosmos, she could barely carry a sentence. Neither had tried to stand since they traveled up the stairs to find a couch.

"Okay. How about we go where we can finish this?" he slurred in a soft attempt at suave.

"I think I better drive; let me go get my car." She stood and wavered for a minute, but put her first stiletto forward then the next. "I think I can get this," she murmured.

He smiled and sat there like a fighter in the corner of the ring after the tenth round. He didn't realize his belt and zipper were undone.

★   ★   ★

Johnson and Jones were done watching and felt like eating a late-night breakfast. Jones' girlfriend had a productive night, and she said she'd meet them later. It was around eleven o'clock and it was packed inside Omar's. At least for the club set, all seemed well with the world.

The rain was coming down in sheets. A spring thunderstorm had arrived and everyone was waiting it out.

Chapter 80

Blair didn't feel like hanging out, not with Parker in the same place. He was convinced she wasn't coming, especially if she knew Parker was here.

"This is bullshit," he said as he stood up and began to walk toward Parker.

Sam was on the dance floor; Parker saw Blair coming. He stood and brought his body square to Blair's. He was ready for a fight, if necessary.

"Hey, I just wanted to say hello and sorry about everything you've gone through," Blair said as he stuck out his hand to shake.

"Ah, yeah. Blair is it?" Parker responded in a relaxed manner.

"Yes. She did the same thing to me, except I hit back. The bitch had me arrested. I never realized until then what you all knew, and I didn't." Blair was anxious to tell all he could as fast as he could.

"When did this happen?" Parker asked.

"Oh, a couple months ago. Dead of winter. She's even got the house, for now. Your furniture, my house, her ex's kids, wow. Do you believe it? You can't make this shit up." Blair sipped his martini and looked at the dance floor.

"Did you say this past winter?"

"Yeah," Blair responded matter-of-factly.

"Was she up north?" Parker was sitting down on the bar stool.

"I don't have a clue. She just came and went as she pleased. I let her. It worked better that way. Why?" Blair nodded at the bartender for another martini.

"I think she's the one who shot me." Parker stared intently at Blair.

"What?" Blair suddenly felt a chill. He looked at Parker as if he had seen a ghost.

"Yup. Sitting in a coffee shop playing cards on a Saturday morning, and crack, down I went. Lucky though. Got me in the chest." The band was loud now. Parker had to lean into Blair to talk. "Once the lung healed it was okay. The bullet had to go through glass and thick clothing. Only thing that saved me, I guess."

"No shit? No way. She always said she was afraid of you." Blair sat his empty martini glass on the bar.

"Afraid? The only thing she's afraid of is running out of money and her ass getting big." Parker smirked.

"Not anymore," said Blair as he reached for a fresh martini. "She's got enough money, and I paid to have her butt lifted." He sipped the martini as he looked away in disgust.

Parker couldn't help but smile and shake his head. Sam was finished dancing and walked over.

"The only way it will end," Parker said, "is when she meets somebody who, well, anyway …"

Chapter 81

Johnson paid their tab and was putting on his coat, waiting for his companion to return from the bathroom. The crowd was thick; he could see Jones struggling to get through.

"All set?" Johnson asked.

"Good. I'm starting to feel like I know too many people. Let's get outta here." Jones smiled and motioned toward the front door.

"We're gone," Johnson quipped as he started to walk.

★   ★   ★

The kid tried to get up but stumbled and realized his pants were at his knees. The people upstairs laughed, pointed, and tried giving him high-fives and fist bumps. He fell and people helped him up. A bouncer came over and finished putting him together. They started to walk down the stairs.

★   ★   ★

"Let's go somewhere quieter," Parker said to Blair and Sam.

"Sure. How about something to eat?" Sam suggested.

"I'm in," Blair said.

"I'll go get the car," said Parker as he walked to the door. Blair went out the back to his car.

As Parker went out the front door of the Exchange, he noticed the black Benz double-parked by the front of the canopy next door at Omar's. A blonde was getting out of the car. He stopped in his tracks.

"Shit," he said.

She turned his way as she closed the car door. She stopped and looked in disbelief. Rain pelted her; she looked like a statue.

The Buick moved quickly from its parking spot. No headlights. No horn. It caught her before she had a chance to move. Her body was caught between the cars and her head smashed against the top of the Benz. As Parker watched in disbelief, the nanoseconds seemed like an hour.

Johnson and Jones came out of Omar's in the instant her body crumpled to the ground. The Buick was well down the road and out of sight. In fact, Johnson didn't realize anything was wrong until he tried to get out from behind one car and around to the front of the Benz. As he looked left, he saw Parker frozen, staring down.

"Parker? What the hell …" Johnson yelled through the rain and wind.

Then he saw a body on the ground next to the Benz. He grabbed Jones and they both rushed to the woman. They could tell instantly she was dead.

The bouncer did his best to open the door and help the kid out. The light was bright under the canopy, but he saw Johnson's head pop up from the top of the cars in front.

"Hey! Call 9-1-1. Now!" Johnson yelled.

The bouncer let go of the kid, who swirled and landed against the hood of the car in front. He sat down and with his back against the front tire, dropped his head by his left shoulder and passed out. The rain drenched him.

"Parker? Hey, where's the car?" Sam yelled as she stepped onto the sidewalk. "Parker?" she screamed as she ran to him. "Oh, my god!"

Parker had not moved. Johnson rushed over to him while Jones stood by the body.

"What happened? What are you doing here?" Johnson was in Parker's face.

"Do you see that?" Parker said.

"No, what? What the hell happened?" Johnson kept staring in Parker's eyes.

"That's her, Johnson. That's *her!*" Parker pointed at the crumpled body.

"*Who?*" Johnson pressed.

"That's the woman who shot me."

Sam ran past them and looked around the cars at Jones, as the first police car arrived. Sparrow Hospital was down the street; Sam could see the EMS unit coming.

Johnson had the palm of his right hand on Parker's left shoulder, shaking him. "What happened? Tell me, now." Rain ran down their faces.

"She just got hit. Smashed like a sandwich between her car and the one driving by." Parker couldn't take his eyes off the body.

"What other car? Did you see what it looked like?" Johnson looked up and down the street. His eyes squinting into the rain.

"No. No, I didn't." Parker still looked down.

With the shock of seeing her, Parker only saw the car's shadow coming out of the light and with the spotlights under the canopy he couldn't tell anything about the car. He and Johnson walked toward the body. Sam bent over the body as the police started to talk with Jones. Blair saw the familiar car and all the commotion when he drove from around back. He parked the Rendezvous and ran over.

"My God." He stopped.

"Do you know her?" asked one of the Lansing police officers.

"That's my wife," he stammered.

The EMS unit had arrived and the paramedics were carefully turning the body and readying their equipment.

"You better call the M.E. She's dead," said the paramedic. "That's brain matter on the ground. She's gone."

The lifeless eyes stayed open as water fell on the bloody, distorted face.

Sam walked over to Parker. She hugged him. Parker looked

down the street as more people gathered and the few cars that were driving by slowed down to gawk.

Parker looked at Sam. He grabbed her face with both hands and whispered, "The car that hit her? I know that car."

★   ★   ★

The Buick drove through traffic unnoticed. Headlights worked. Parking light on the passenger side worked. No dents. Perfect. The driver remained calm as the car headed east on I-96.

Good night was the outgoing text on the phone.

★   ★   ★

After the verification of the text, the room deep under the NSA in Fort Meade was silent. Six people sat back in their chairs; some had their arms stretched over their heads. One person yawned. The only woman in the room placed a strikethrough on the next name and sent a reply text:

Good night

About the Author

After working as a professional, educator, executive and lobbyist in health care for thirty-eight years, Stewert James lives a quiet life of volunteering and consulting in Northern Michigan.